A Christmas Marriage

DALLAS SCHULZE

SILHOUETTE
Sensation

First published in Great Britain in 1994
by Silhouette Books, Eton House, 18-24 Paradise Road,
Richmond, Surrey TW9 1SR

ISBN 0 373 59275 2

95-9411

Made and printed in Great Britain

Chapter One

They'd had a Christmas wedding and a Halloween divorce. That was what Tess Armstrong always said if the subject of her brief marriage came up. It was a light, breezy answer, perfectly suited to turning away any probing questions. Not that very many people would have asked probing questions anyway, not in Southern California. If there was one thing Southern Californians understood besides how to get the perfect tan, it was how to mind their own business.

But on the off chance that the questioner was too new to the area to understand the unwritten social laws that governed the famous laid-back life-style, Tess's casual reply made it sound as if the subject of her marriage was simply not interesting enough to pursue.

Sometimes, she almost managed to convince herself that the five years that had passed since the divorce had put her marriage in the distant and nearly forgotten past. Weeks would go by when she didn't even think about her ex-husband. If asked about him, she might even have taken a moment to recall his face.

Tess was proud of the distance she'd managed to put between herself and her youthful marriage. It had taken her years to achieve that indifference.

It only took a moment to show her just how thin a facade it really was.

AS USUAL, FRAN invited twice as many people as her house could accommodate, on the theory that most of them wouldn't show up. As usual, most of them showed up. Fran and Charlie McKenzie's parties were always worth attending, for the spectacular views from their hilltop home and for the interesting mix of guests. You could find yourself talking to anyone from a state senator to a garbage collector who just happened to do watercolors that Fran admired. And if smog obscured the lights of the city or the guests happened to be a dull batch, there was always the food.

Fran's Food was generally acknowledged to be one of the city's best catering services. And Fran always catered her own parties. "It's good for business,'' she said, whenever someone suggested that she worked as hard on her own parties as she did on her clients'. ''Besides, I can hardly hire the competition, now can I?''

She might not hire the competition, but she was perfectly capable of inviting them to the party, along with anyone else who happened to catch her endlessly roving eye.

Tess leaned against the balcony railing and watched the ebb and flow of people moving through the open balcony doors. Half-shielded by a potted ficus tree that towered over her head, she was free to observe without being noticed, which suited her just fine. It was August and the temperature still hovered at seventy, despite the fact that the sun had set a couple of hours before. In typical fashion, the party had expanded onto the balcony and into the gardens beyond. Guests strolled along strategically lit pathways and sat on cushioned wrought-iron benches, balancing plates of food on their knees.

Tess had already nibbled to her heart's content and now she was indulging in one of her favorite entertainments—people watching. And she could always count on Fran to provide plenty of interesting people to watch.

The woman stepping through the balcony doors, for example. From the top of her artfully tousled, pseudo sun-streaked hair to the tips of her three-inch scarlet pumps, she was the picture of casual sophistication. She looked like an actress or perhaps a model. Nothing else could justify that exquisitely lean body and the taut skin that owed as much to a scalpel as it did to genes. As it happened, Tess recognized her. The woman owned a construction company, one she'd built from the ground up, and she was just as comfortable with a hammer in her hand as she was cradling a wineglass.

Behind her was a perennial loser in the political sweepstakes. He was a candidate in every election and he consistently lost by a landslide. Tess had never been able to decide whether she admired his determination or deplored his inability to take a hint.

And standing just behind him . . .

Tess's fingers clenched around the stem of her wineglass as shock washed over her.

Nick.

It didn't matter that she could see only the thick wave of dark blond hair and the angle of his jaw. She would have known him anywhere, even if all she could see was the back of his head. No one else stood like that, feet slightly apart, broad shoulders squared, one hand hidden in the pocket of his tailored gray trousers. She'd once teased him, saying that he looked as if he were standing on the bridge of a ship, feet braced against the motion of the water, shoulders braced against any gale that might blow.

He'd laughed and called her "my pretty" as he swept her into his arms. With a comic leer, he'd said that of all the booty he'd captured, she was the prize piece. The scene had ended in bed, which was the one place their marriage had never had a problem.

Tess swallowed hard and forced the memories away, shifting her eyes from Nick's back at the same time. She hadn't seen him since the divorce, hadn't thought of him in months. Yet all it took was a glimpse of him to bring the memories tumbling back.

Why hadn't Fran warned her?

Because she knew Tess wouldn't have come if she'd been told Nick was to be there.

Out of the corner of her eye, she saw him turning toward the balcony doors. On a surge of pure panic, Tess turned and pretended absorption in the sprawl of glowing lights that was Los Angeles. *Idiot.* What was the matter with her? She was hiding from Nick as if he were the bogeyman. She eased closer to the ficus, wishing there were a nice, dense hedge she could hide behind.

It was just the shock of seeing him after so long, she told herself. As soon as she recovered her balance, she would turn and act like the mature adult she was. With luck, Nick wouldn't even notice her as she scuttled for the door.

"Tess?" The low voice stroked over her skin, as if he'd trailed fingers the length of her spine, most of which was left bare by the halter dress she wore.

For a split second, she considered the possibility of diving over the railing into the shrubbery beneath, but she was sure that didn't appear in any handbooks about how to react to seeing your ex-husband. Instead, she drew a deep breath, and forced her mouth to curve in a smile as she turned to face the man she'd once loved more than life.

"Nick! What a surprise." The tone was a little too hearty but her voice was steady. "I didn't see you," she added, just in case he thought his presence had anything to do with her position behind the ficus. Casually she edged away from the sheltering foliage.

"I just got here a few minutes ago. I bumped into Charlie at the airport and he insisted on dragging me home with him. Said Fran was throwing a party. He brings home stray puppies, too, I understand."

Tess laughed at the small joke, even as she was thinking that Nick Masters had about as much in common with a stray puppy as a cougar did with a calico kitten.

Was it possible he'd gotten even handsomer in the last five years? Or was it just that she'd managed to convince herself that he wasn't as impossibly good-looking as she'd remembered?

"How have you been?" he asked. "You look terrific."

Tess told herself that his look of masculine approval had absolutely no affect on her. The goose bumps popping up on her shoulders must have been caused by a stray breeze.

"Thank you. You look good yourself."

"Good" was an anemic description. "Good" didn't begin to describe the way the light caught in the heavy gold of his thick hair. Tess's fingers tightened around her wineglass.

"Thanks." Nick's smile softened, his eyes warm. "How are you, Tess?"

"I'm fine." Her voice sounded too tight and she took a quick sip of wine. Damn him! Why did he have to look just as she'd remembered? Why couldn't he have gone bald and developed a potbelly? Better yet, why couldn't he have gotten glasses? They might have helped to conceal those emerald green eyes that had always seemed to look right into her soul.

"I hear your shop is doing well," Nick said, when it became clear she wasn't going to say anything more.

"From whom?" The words came out sharper than she'd intended. She saw Nick's eyes widen in surprise and felt a flush come up in her cheeks. "I wouldn't think you'd have much interest in a tiny little place like mine," she added, lifting one shoulder in a half shrug.

"I was always interested in what you did," he reminded her quietly.

And he had been, Tess admitted to herself. He hadn't been one of those men who talked about what happened at work and never thought to ask how their wives had spent their day. Nick had always asked. The problem was, she'd never had anything to tell him.

"The shop is fine," she said, sidestepping the question of his interest. "I've been lucky."

"I doubt luck had much to do with it. Small businesses don't succeed on luck."

"Well, I've put in a lot of hours," she admitted, wishing she didn't feel such a response to the admiration in his eyes. ''How is the architecture business these days? Still traveling all over the country?''

Nick was the star architect in the firm his grandfather had founded. Masters Architectural designed everything from office buildings to private homes. During their brief marriage, he'd spent two weeks of every month away from home, meeting with clients, supervising projects, examining building sites, doing all the things that went along with maintaining the firm's reputation for quality.

She'd traveled with him at first, but after a few months, the novelty of life in a series of hotel rooms had worn thin and she'd started staying home when he left.

''I'm doing a lot less traveling these days,'' Nick said. ''Hope joined the firm two years ago and she does quite a bit of the traveling.''

''I thought Hope was determined to do noble deeds. Wasn't she thinking about joining the Peace Corps or something like that?''

''She gave that idea up when she found out she might have to live without flush toilets.''

Tess chuckled, trying to imagine the exquisite Hope Masters roughing it in the bush. ''I guess nobility only goes so far.''

"Well, she hasn't given up entirely. She talked my father into taking on several low-income housing projects. I think it makes her feel less of a traitor when she finds herself working on a ten-thousand-square-foot mansion."

"How are your parents? And Annie and Sara?" His family was a safe topic—and she was groping for one, desperately trying not to let her eyes linger on her ex-husband's face. Anyway, she'd been fond of her in-laws and she'd honestly missed them after the divorce. She felt her face flush with heat. There was only one other thing she missed more....

NICK WAS WILLING to give her updates on his family if that was what she wanted. The tension had eased from her face, her eyes didn't look quite so panicked.

Five years, he thought, his eyes going over her. She'd been only twenty when they separated. She'd been pretty then, with a youthful softness that had brought out his protective instincts. In the past few years she'd lost the last traces of girlishness and matured into a beautiful woman.

The changes were subtle. At twenty-five, her skin was still smooth as silk, all sun-warmed peach tones that glowed against the sapphire blue of her dress. The halter-style top revealed most of her shoulders and he found himself wanting to trace his fingers over the delicate line of her collarbone, wanting to see if that light touch would make her tremble the way it once had.

Her hair was coiled into a smooth chignon at the back of her head. Raven's-wing black, it was thick and straight. He remembered it tumbled over her shoulders, the morning sun picking out blue highlights, her neck arched with pleasure as they made love. Had she cut it or did it still fall to her waist in a shining black curtain?

He glanced away, swallowing hard against the sudden wave of hunger that swept over him. It was a good thing he was wearing loosely tailored trousers and not tight jeans, he thought ruefully. It had been a long time since he'd become aroused just looking at a woman. Since the divorce, he thought. Since the last time he'd seen Tess.

One of the other guests had joined them and was asking Tess something about her shop. Nick let his mind drift from the conversation and his eyes drift over his ex-wife. God, but she looked good. How could he have forgotten how beautiful she was? How desirable? He had only to look at her to find himself growing hard. It had always been like that. From the first moment he'd seen her, he'd wanted her.

They'd met at a Halloween party. Tess had been dressed as a black cat. Wearing a black leotard, a ridiculous black velvet tail, with penciled whiskers on her cheeks and a headband with ears on her head, she'd looked at once sensuous and innocent. And Nick had wanted her more than he'd ever wanted a woman in his life.

It had taken him less than a week to convince her to sleep with him and no one had been more surprised than he was when he found himself proposing the next morning. Tess had refused, telling him that he was just feeling guilty because he'd been her first lover. But it hadn't been guilt he'd felt. It had been a soul-deep hunger, a need to tie her to him as solidly as he could, to make her his in every way possible. Making love to her wasn't enough.

It had taken him almost two months to convince her to marry him and he was willing to admit that he hadn't played completely fair. He hadn't hesitated to use sex as a persuader, tumbling her into bed whenever she started to argue about how little time they'd known each other.

After they were married, their sex life had been everything he'd fantasized it would be. That was one place they'd never had any problems with their marriage. No matter what else had gone wrong, *that* had been right—more right than it had been either before or since.

And in the last five years, he thought, he'd almost managed to make himself forget just how right it had been.

"It's good to see you, Tess," he said abruptly, as soon as the guest had taken her leave. He saw her eyes widen, saw surprise and some other emotion he couldn't identify, and then her lashes lowered, concealing the sapphire blue of her eyes.

"It's good to see you, too, Nick." But her tone made the words nothing more than a polite response, telling him nothing of how she really felt.

That had been one of the most frustrating aspects of their marriage—the way she had of concealing what she was feeling, of saying what she thought he wanted to hear, not what she really thought. And he'd learned then that the harder he pushed, the deeper she retreated into that polite little shell. It had gotten to the point where he'd had to fight the urge to grab her and shake her until the shell cracked, revealing the emotions inside.

"I've missed you." The words tumbled out before he could censor them.

The startled way her eyes swept up to his made him wish the words unsaid. He was going too fast. Again. Just as he'd done when he met her, sweeping her into marriage without giving her a chance to think about it. Hadn't he learned his lesson then?

He scrambled to cover up his blunt remark. "I haven't had a decent apple pie in five years," he said, and added a sly grin.

The subtle tension in her eyes seemed to ease and her mouth curved in a smile. "You always did have a sweet tooth."

"It's still there."

An awkward silence fell between them. Nick thought of half a dozen things he wanted to ask. He wanted to know if she ever thought about the time they'd had together, if she ever regretted the divorce. Was there still an empty place inside her when she thought about him? Was she dating? Did she have a lover?

His chest felt tight and hard at the thought of Tess in bed with another man. Not jealousy, certainly. He was long past the stage where he was jealous of her. But he was willing to admit to a certain possessiveness, a foolish male reluctance to share something that had once been his.

"I think Fran needs some help," she said suddenly, looking past his shoulder.

Nick didn't bother to turn. He knew as well as she did that Fran's parties always ran like clockwork. He also knew that Fran would rather tap-dance nude down Wilshire Boulevard than ask one of her guests to help.

"Maybe we could get together and have a cup of coffee somewhere," he said, reluctant to let her walk away. Nostalgia, he told himself. He was just feeling nostalgic.

The suggestion brought Tess's eyes back to his face. For just an instant, he thought he saw something there, a look that said his words had touched some chord of response. But then it was gone, her expression shuttered against him.

"I don't think that's a good idea, Nick." Her eyes met his for an instant before sliding away. "It was nice to see you," she murmured. She slipped past him without waiting for his response.

Nick didn't try to stop her. He stayed where she'd left him, one hand cradling an untouched glass of Scotch, his eyes on the spectacular view of the city. But he wasn't seeing the sprawl of lights. He was seeing a pair of sapphire blue eyes. And wondering if he'd imagined that brief moment when they seemed to reflect an emptiness that matched his own.

TESS RESISTED THE URGE to walk away from Nick and straight out the front door. That would look as if she was running away. And even though that was exactly what she wanted to do, pride demanded she stay at least long enough to show she'd taken the meeting in stride.

She chatted with casual acquaintances, laughed at the right times and tried not to be too obvious about keeping tabs on Nick's whereabouts. Since Fran's house sprawled over the hillside and the party spilled not only into every room but out into the gardens, it was all but impossible to keep track of any one person, especially while trying to appear completely disinterested.

But she did see Nick several times. He seemed to be having a great time, she thought resentfully. Watching him talk to a long-legged busty blonde, she found herself wondering if he even remembered that his ex-wife was here. The blonde leaned forward to say something to him, practically nibbling his ear in the process, her breast pressed intimately against the sleeve of his dark jacket. Nick didn't appear to have any objections to having a strange woman all but plaster herself to his side.

Of course, maybe she wasn't a stranger. The thought created an odd pinched sensation in Tess's chest and she turned away. Who was or wasn't a stranger to Nick was not her concern anymore. When she'd asked for a divorce, she'd given up the right to feel jealous because another woman had her hand on his arm.

IT WAS ALMOST ELEVEN before Tess decided she could leave without anyone being able to say her departure had anything to do with her ex-husband. She located Fran and said her farewells, thankful that Fran was occupied with her duties as hostess and didn't have time to offer more than a token protest at Tess's somewhat early departure.

As she headed for the door, Tess looked for Nick, uncertain whether she hoped to see him or not. Part of her craved another glimpse of him, while another more cautious part suggested it would be better if she didn't see him.

He was not in sight and she tried to feel relieved. She'd said her goodbyes five years ago. There was no need to say them again.

Since the McKenzie home was perched on a hilltop, the driveway to it was steep. There were no stairs leading down to the street. As Fran put it, this way they knew that anyone who made the climb *really* wanted to see them. Tess hesitated at the top of the slope and then reached down to slip off her high-heeled sandals, glad she'd decided against wearing hose.

The concrete held a day's accumulation of sun and it felt warm against her bare feet. Her shoes dangling from her fingers, she made her way down the drive, grateful for the soft illumination provided by the low lamps that lined the drive. Her car was parked at the bottom of the hill, a pale blue compact wedged between a silver Mercedes and a rusty pickup truck. She smiled, thinking that the three cars were a perfect metaphor for Fran's eclectic guest list.

She had just pulled her keys from her purse when she heard someone call her name. Her fingers tightened over the keys.

Nick.

She turned reluctantly toward the sound of his voice, watching him negotiate the steep drive at a speed far greater than her own cautious descent.

"I'm glad I caught you," he said, as he reached the street level and started toward her.

"Why?" Despite herself, Tess felt her pulse pick up speed. Half a dozen possibilities flashed through her mind, ranging from he wanted to beg her to come back to him to he wanted to tell her he was getting married again.

"Could you give me a lift home?"

"Home?" She stared at him blankly for a moment. Home to the house they'd shared for eighteen months? The house he'd given her in the settlement? The one that still occasionally reminded her of him so strongly that she sometimes thought it would be better to sell it to finally escape the memories?

"My condo," Nick clarified. "I caught a ride from the airport with Charlie and I hate to ask him to leave his own party to take me home. It's not far out of your way."

"I don't know, Nick...." Her voice trailed off as she sought, and failed to find, a good reason for refusing his request.

"I'm not asking for a loan, Tess. Just a ride." Nick's tone gently chided her hesitation, making her feel foolish.

"Sure." Her agreement sounded anything but gracious. Was it because she resented feeling manipulated...or because she resented the quick flare of pleasure that came with the thought of spending more time with her ex-husband?

Tess didn't care to answer.

Chapter Two

Nick folded his long legs into the passenger seat, guiltily aware of the car keys in his pocket. He'd never been a man inclined to easy lies, whether in business or in his personal life. But when he'd seen Tess leaving the party, he'd had the sudden feeling that he couldn't just let her walk out.

He'd watched her all evening without seeming to do so. The memories of the girl who'd been his wife were already blurred by the reality of the woman she'd become. He found himself wanting the woman she was even more than he'd wanted her before. The deep hunger he remembered seemed sharper, more demanding than it had been five years ago. He simply couldn't let her walk away.

So he'd left the party without bothering to say good-night to his hosts, followed his ex-wife and lied shamelessly to her. Glancing sideways, he saw her profile against the window—long forehead, short straight nose, the soft pout of her mouth.

And he felt no regret at his prevarication.

TESS WAS VIVIDLY AWARE of Nick's large presence. She'd thought he was too close at Fran's party but the compact car made them positively cozy. Why hadn't she bought a van? Or better yet, a bus? A nice, big bus where Nick could have been seated at least twenty feet away.

He shifted, trying to find a more comfortable position. The little car hadn't been designed with a man of his size in mind. His leg was only inches from hers. In the pale blue light from the dashboard, she could see the way the crease in his trouser leg flattened over his bent knee. Nick had been a runner when she knew him and she'd sometimes teased him that he had better legs than she did. She didn't have to close her eyes to remember what he looked like in running shorts.

Or what he looked like without them. Tess swallowed hard and forced her thoughts in other, safer, directions. But she felt her breath catch when his hand settled on the back of her seat. He was just trying to get comfortable, she told herself. The fact that his fingers were nearly touching her hair was pure coincidence. It didn't mean he was remembering the way he'd always pulled the pins from her hair so it would spill over his hands, or the way he'd tangle his fingers in it when they made love, holding her head beneath his, his eyes intent on her face, watching her response.

"So, you bought a condo." The words were abrupt, a little forced, her voice higher than normal. Too revealing, she thought, too obvious that she wanted—needed—to break the silence.

"Yeah. I didn't feel like getting a house, not just for myself."

His words brought the memories flooding back—the two of them looking at the old house in Pasadena for the first time, Nick pointing out that it needed a lot of work, her wrapping her hands around his upper arm and telling him to stop looking with his mind, and listen with his heart. The house *needed* them. It needed someone to buy it and take care of it, restore it to its former glory. Besides, there was a huge sycamore in the backyard that practically cried out to have a bench set under it. Nick had muttered that the tree cried out to have a chain saw taken to it, but he'd given in and admitted that the place *did* have some possibilities.

She didn't have to look at him to know he was remembering the same things: the midnight wallpapering sessions, the miles of trim they'd stripped by hand, removing nearly a hundred years' worth of paint to reveal the beautiful wood beneath.

"You could have had the house," Tess said into the silence.

"No. It meant a lot to you. You're still there?"

"Yes." She flipped on a turn signal and eased her way off the freeway. She didn't add anything to the flat statement. She certainly couldn't tell him that there were still moments when she turned, half expecting to see him in a doorway, his thick blond hair spattered with paint, demanding that she come and help him with some task. After all, he'd say, she was the one who'd wanted this white elephant. As if he hadn't wanted the place too, the moment he saw it.

The remainder of the drive was silent, broken only by Nick's quiet directions. Strangely, it wasn't an uncomfortable silence. The sharing of memories, even if unacknowledged, seemed to have eased the tension. Maybe it was the idea that something concrete had come from their marriage, even if it was only the restoration of an old house.

TESS PULLED THE CAR to a stop in front of the building Nick indicated. In the darkness, the row of condos was visible only as sharply angled rooflines against the night sky. When Nick didn't move to get out of the car, she shut the engine off. The sudden silence was almost deafening.

"Come in for a nightcap," Nick said, turning his head to look at her.

Tess shook her head, even as she felt a little leap of something that could have been—but wasn't—anticipation.

"I'm driving."

"Then come in for a cup of coffee."

"It's late."

"Decaffeinated."

"I shouldn't."

"Fresh ground," he coaxed, sensing she was weakening.

"Really, I shouldn't." It wasn't the coffee that tempted her, fresh ground or otherwise. And that was why she couldn't take him up on his offer. The last thing she needed was to let Nick Masters back into her life, even just the tiny bit necessary to share a cup of coffee with him.

"I'm not going to bite, Tess." The trace of amusement in his voice brought her chin up a fraction.

"I'm not afraid of you," she said. *Only of myself.*

"Then come in for coffee. Please, Tess. I'd like to talk to you." His hand still lay on her seat and he shifted it now, brushing the back of his fingers against her cheek.

Tess felt the light touch all the way to her toes. She kept her gaze lowered, not wanting Nick to see her reaction, knowing he'd already sensed it. It had always been like that between them, the awareness that needed only the barest touch to spring to life. *That* was why she wasn't going to accept his invitation. *That* was why she was going to issue a polite refusal, see him out of her car and drive away without a backward glance. It had taken her five years to put her life back together. She wasn't going to let Nick Masters back into it, not even by the smallest amount.

"A cup of coffee does sound good."

THE CONDOMINIUMS WERE SET against the foothills above Glendale. The view drew a murmur of appreciation from Tess when Nick pulled open the drapes in the living room.

"It's not as spectacular as the view Fran and Charlie have, but it's not bad," Nick commented as he tugged open the sliding glass door and gestured her through onto the narrow balcony. "The whole building really should be turned about ten degrees for the best advantage," he added critically.

"Obviously it's not a Masters design. A Masters design would have been perfect." The teasing comment surprised Tess even as she said it.

"Actually, it *isn't* one of ours." Nick leaned one hip against the redwood railing. "*I* would have found a way to take advantage of the view." The tuck in his cheek made a joke of his haughty tone.

"Naturally." Tess set her hands on the railing and settled her gaze on the sparkling lights below. It seemed like a hundred years ago that she'd been looking at a similar view from Fran's balcony. Before she'd known Nick was at the party, before she'd had reason to remember the way he could make her tingle all over with just a look.

Nick cocked his head as the kettle began to whistle. He'd found the coffee and set the water to boil before showing her the view.

"The water's ready. I'll go pour it over the grounds."

Tess nodded. She closed her eyes as he went back into the living room. This was crazy. What was she doing in Nick's condo, pretending to admire the view? The only view she could see at the moment was emerald green eyes and a pair of shoulders where she'd once rested her head.

She opened her eyes and turned restlessly away from the view, moving back into the living room.

A heavy pottery lamp cast a circle of light onto the thick black carpet and lit one side of the curved gray sofa. The black-and-gray color scheme was softened by splashes of mauve. It was a sophisticated look. A bachelor's look, she thought and then told herself she didn't feel a stab of pain when she thought of Nick as a bachelor.

"Jamaican Blue Mountain. Freshly ground, with just a spoonful of cream." At Nick's words, Tess turned toward him.

Her breath caught in her throat in involuntary reaction. He'd discarded his suit jacket and tie. The sleeves of his pearl gray Egyptian cotton shirt were rolled up to reveal his muscled forearms and the top two buttons were undone, allowing a glimpse of the mat of dark blond hair that covered his chest.

Tess's palms tingled with the memory of how that crisp hair felt against her fingers, under her palm. She could see the ripple of muscle under the fine cotton and she felt an answering ripple of response in the pit of her stomach.

"Tess?" She blinked and dragged her eyes from Nick's chest to his face. "Something wrong?"

"No." Her voice was hardly more than a whisper and she cleared her throat and tried again. "No. My mind was just wandering."

"No law against it." She was grateful he didn't question just where her mind might have wandered. But as she took the cup from him, their eyes met and she had the uneasy feeling he knew exactly where her thoughts had gone.

The coffee was smooth and rich. Nick was the one who'd taught her that coffee could be something to be savored rather than merely consumed. After the divorce, she'd gone back to instant and she'd nearly forgotten just how good coffee could taste.

"You could have bought a grinder," Nick responded when she said as much. "If I'd known you were going to go back to swill, I'd have left mine."

"Swill seems a bit extreme," she protested, obeying his gestured suggestion to sit on the sofa. As she sank into the thick gray leather, it occurred to her that she'd never imagined the time would come when either of them would be able to make casual references to their divorce, to the painful process of dividing their lives.

"Trust me, swill is a compliment."

Tess's fingers tightened around her cup as Nick sank onto the sofa. She'd expected him to take one of the chairs, where he'd be at a nice, safe distance. But the sofa was placed to offer a good view of the city lights, so it didn't seem unreasonable that Nick should choose to sit there.

What did seem unreasonable was the way her pulse accelerated at his nearness. It was the same reaction he'd always inspired in her, the reason she'd let him seduce her into his bed, the reason she'd married him. But it wasn't enough to build a relationship on, she reminded herself. Her pulse ignored her, continuing to beat too quickly.

"It really is a beautiful view," she said, trying to distract herself from the direction her thoughts were going.

"I like it."

But when she glanced at Nick, he wasn't looking at the view. His gaze was on her, searching, questioning. Tess reached up to touch her hair in a self-conscious gesture.

"Is my hair coming down or do I have a smudge on my nose?"

"Sorry. I didn't mean to stare." But he didn't look away. "I was just thinking that you've changed."

"It's been five years. Most people change in five years." Needing something to do with her hands, she reached out to set her cup down on the low glass table that sat in front of the sofa.

"Most people don't get more beautiful."

The husky words made Tess's eyes jerk to his. And what she read there ended any hope she had of making her pulse behave.

"Nick..."

"When I saw you at the party, all I could think of was that you'd become even more beautiful than you were five years ago."

"Nick..." His hand came up, his fingers delving into the soft chignon.

She was going to move away, Tess told herself. She was going to stand up and tell him that she hadn't come here to be seduced by him. She was going to walk out with her pride—not to mention her virtue—intact.

He pulled the pins out and her hair spilled over his hand like heavy black silk.

"You didn't cut it," he whispered, watching it ripple past her waist.

"No." Tess swallowed hard, her skin flushing at the look in his eyes. It was that remembered look—the remembered hunger—that had stopped her every time she decided to get her hair cut into some short-and-sassy style.

"I used to dream about the way you looked," Nick said softly. He curled his fingers deeper into her hair as his eyes lifted to hers. "After the divorce, I wanted to forget you. But at night, when I closed my eyes, I'd remember the way you'd look when we made love, wearing nothing but that black cape of hair. And me."

Tess couldn't drag her eyes from his. She was going to put an end to this scene. She was going to walk away before she did something incredibly stupid. Like let herself be seduced by the look in her ex-husband's eyes.

Nick's thumb brushed over the sensitive skin beneath her ear and she forgot how to breathe.

"Nick..." She started to twist her head away from his touch and found herself leaning into it instead.

"You used to say my name just that way when we made love. All breathless and hungry."

When had he gotten so close? She could see the faint gold lines that radiated out from his pupils, giving depth to the dark green. The hunger in his eyes made it hard to breathe, made it impossible to think.

"I can't," she whispered, shivering as he trailed his fingers down the length of her throat.

"This was inevitable, Tess. You know it. I know it. It has to happen."

"We're divorced." He was tracing the edge of her halter top, his fingertips almost touching the side of her breast. Tess felt her breast swell in anticipation of that touch. If he looked, she knew Nick would be able to see the shameless invitation of her nipple thrusting against the soft silk of her dress.

"I want you, Tess. And you want me." Without taking his eyes from her, he cupped her breast in one wide palm. Shock dried Tess's mouth. Hunger made her eyes dilate. With just that light touch, he'd rolled back the clock. *This* was what she'd spent five years forgetting. *This* was what she'd never be able to forget.

"We can't." Her fingers closed around his wrist but her strength ended there. She couldn't find the will to push him away.

"We can." Nick's thumb brushed over her swollen nipple and this time she knew he felt the shiver that ran through her. He brought his free hand up, his fingers circling her wrist as he carried her hand to his chest. He pressed her hand flat against his shirt and Tess could feel the heavy beat of his heart beneath her palm. The rhythm was quick and hard, matching her own pulse.

"This isn't what I came here for," she whispered, lifting her eyes to his face.

"Isn't it?" he asked huskily. "Admit it, Tess. You want this as much as I do. Don't turn away from it. I need you."

The three words struck deep. He needed her. He'd always needed her in this way. The tragedy had been that he hadn't needed her on any other level. But that didn't stop her visceral response to that simple declaration.

"Oh, Nick." The words were half protest and all surrender.

"Tess." Her name was a caress. His hand shifted, sliding beneath the silk of her halter-style bodice.

Tess was helpless to stop the soft moan that escaped her, betraying her need. His hand was warm and hard. Nick was as likely to be found with a hammer in his hand as he was a drafting tool and his callused skin abraded her tender flesh in a way that made breathing require a conscious effort.

He caught her nipple between thumb and forefinger, and she swayed toward him like a flower bending in the wind. Her fingertips flexed against his chest and her eyelids half closed as she savored the feel of him touching her, holding her.

It had been so long. She must have murmured the words aloud or perhaps Nick read her mind.

"Too long, Tess. Much too long." Without moving his hand from her breast, he set his other hand on the back of her neck, drawing her closer.

Tess told herself she was going to tell him this had to stop. Here and now. Before they did something she was going to regret. They were opening a door that had been closed a long time, and behind that door lay a great deal of pain. But so much pleasure, too, she thought, her eyes closing as Nick's mouth hovered over hers.

There was nothing tentative in his kiss. He was a man kissing a woman with whom he'd been intimate, a woman who'd shared his bed for nearly two years. He knew her, knew her responses as intimately as he knew his own. His tongue traced the softness of her lower lip before sliding past the barrier of her teeth and into the honeyed sweetness of her mouth. Tess could taste the smoky darkness of coffee on his tongue. Or was it on hers? It didn't matter. It wasn't possible to tell where one began and the other ended. There was only the two of them, joined together, just the way they were meant to be.

NICK TASTED HER SURRENDER in the way her fingers clutched his shirt in pleading little handfuls, in the ripe swell of her breast in his hand, in the eager way her tongue met his, teasing him deeper.

He hadn't consciously planned this when he'd asked her to come in for coffee. He'd told himself he only wanted to talk to her, perhaps to find some footing between them besides the old hurts they shared. But looking at her in the shadowy lamplight, her eyes deep, mysterious pools, her mouth full and soft, all he'd been able to think about was how desperately he wanted her. There'd never been another woman who'd made him ache the way he did for Tess.

Kissing her, he felt like a man dying of thirst who'd just been given a drink of cool, clear water. Only there was nothing cool about the way she made him feel. He felt the way he'd always felt with her, hot and hungry and in danger of forgetting that he was a man of thirty-eight, not a randy teenager.

He fumbled at the back of her neck, finding the soft bow that held her bodice up and tugging it loose. Tess gasped something against his mouth—a protest, approval—he didn't know which. And then the peacock blue silk slipped to her waist.

Nick dragged his mouth from hers to look down at the treasure he'd uncovered. Tess murmured an embarrassed protest, her hands shifting as if to cover herself. He caught her wrists.

"You're so beautiful, Tess. So damned beautiful." He released his hold on her wrists and Tess shivered as his hands came up to cup her full breasts, lifting them. Unable to resist the temptation they presented, he bent his head over her, taking one swollen nipple into his mouth, tasting her.

TESS FELT THE STRENGTH drain from her legs as he sucked strongly at her breast. She felt the pressure deep inside, a burning need that hovered on the knife-edge of pain.

God, it had been so long. So very long.

Her fingers delved into the heavy gold of his hair, pulling him closer as she arched her back to offer herself to him. From the moment she'd seen Nick, she'd known this was how the evening had to end. Not consciously, but on some visceral level she hadn't wanted to acknowledge, she'd known.

She'd been running from the knowledge when she left the party early, denying it when she refused his invitation to come in for coffee. But she was tired of running, no longer interested in denial.

"Nick." His name was a moan. A plea. An admission of hunger.

Nick's mouth abandoned her breast but only to capture her sweet whimper of protest. His tongue stabbed into her mouth, claiming it as his own. His palm flattened against her spine, pulling her closer.

But it wasn't enough. He needed her laid out beneath him, her slender body molded to his, every inch of her bared to his touch.

Tess's eyes opened in dazed surprise as Nick dragged his mouth from hers and rose from the sofa. For an instant, he loomed over her, big and powerful, making her feel small and fragile and a little helpless. Before the feeling could overwhelm the sensual daze, he bent and scooped her off the sofa, lifting her against his chest as if her weight were nothing to him.

His mouth caught hers, smothering her gasp of surprise. And if Tess had thought to offer a protest, it was burned away by the heat of his kiss. He carried her across the living room and into a short hallway illuminated by a wall sconce that sent a splash of light upward against the plaster. Without taking his mouth from hers, Nick kicked open a lacquered black door and carried her into a dimly lit bedroom.

When he set her on her feet beside the bed, Tess's knees threatened to buckle beneath her. She clung to him, pressing her forehead against his chest, feeling the ragged rise and fall of his breathing. The unevenness of his pulse was oddly reassuring. It told her that she wasn't the only one slipping out of control.

"Tess." Her name was a husky whisper, Nick's breath stirring the soft tendrils of hair that lay on her forehead.

She lifted her head to look up at him, her eyes wide and uncertain. The room was dimly lit by a black porcelain lamp that sat on the sleek built-in dresser, but there was enough light to let her see the green fire that burned in Nick's eyes.

"If this isn't what you want, tell me now." The words were clearly not offered without cost. She could feel the hunger in him. It was the same hunger she felt, the same need.

She should tell him to let her go, she thought dimly. Sanity demanded the words. She was only going to end up hurt again. But that hurt seemed a distant, unimportant thing when compared to the ache she felt now. To the need that burned in both of them.

Her hands slid up to his shoulders. She let her body sway into his, her bare breasts pressing against the thin fabric of his shirt.

"You talk too much," she whispered, tilting her head to trail teasing kisses along the hard line of his jaw.

With a laugh that was half a groan, Nick wrapped his arms around her, lifting her off her feet, crushing her so close that not even a shadow could have come between them. His mouth caught hers, telling her without words how much he wanted her.

With that kiss, Tess consciously blocked out everything but the here and now. Nothing mattered beyond this. The future would come and she might pay a price for tonight, but she wasn't going to think about that now. She refused to think of anything but the pleasure of Nick's hands on her body, the sweet torment of need that throbbed in the pit of her stomach.

Her zipper slid downward without a protest. Nick set his hands on her hips, sweeping the dress down, taking her panties with it. Her shoes had vanished somewhere in the living room and she now stood before him completely naked. Any self-consciousness she might have felt was burned away by the green fire of his gaze as it swept over her, devouring her, telling her without words how much he wanted her.

NICK FELT THE IMPACT of Tess's beauty strike deep in his gut. *This* was the image he'd never been able to forget. The hunger he'd never completely lost.

He reached out and caught a handful of her hair, pulling it over her shoulder so that it draped over her breast. The contrast of her black hair against the ivory of her skin was another thing he'd never forgotten.

"You are so beautiful."

"And you are overdressed." Her fingers were trembling as she unbuttoned his shirt. Nick tugged it loose from his pants and shrugged it off, tossing it behind him. His hands closed over her waist, pulling her forward until the taut peaks of her breasts brushed against the hair-roughened surface of his chest. At the contact, a soft moan tore from her. The sound went straight to Nick's gut, tearing away the last fragile layer of patience to expose the raw hunger beneath.

Tess gasped as she was swept up in his arms and set on the bed. The cool linen sheets did nothing to cool her heated skin. She watched from beneath heavy lids as Nick jerked open his belt. The rasp of his zipper being lowered shivered over her skin like a physical touch. He shoved his trousers down over his lean hips, taking the plain white cotton briefs with them. Looking up at him, Tess felt her breath catch.

Stripped of the veneer of clothing, he looked powerfully male. Six feet two inches of corded muscle and tanned skin. He was all hard angles and hunger, and his arousal was blatant.

"Doubts, Tess?" The question brought her eyes to his face. All she had to do was say yes and he'd back away. He'd leave her alone in his bed. Alone, where she'd been for five long years. Tonight, she didn't want to be alone.

"No doubts." She lifted her arms and he came to her.

The heavy weight of him was familiar. Familiar and welcome. Her legs opened to him, her breath catching in a quiet moan as she felt his hips slide between her thighs, felt the hard, silken pressure of him against her.

"Tess." Her name was a whisper, a command. "Look at me," he ordered huskily. She forced her eyelids up as Nick levered himself up on his arms. His eyes burned down into hers, fierce and demanding. "I want to watch you. I want to watch your eyes as you take me inside you."

She wanted to close her eyes, turn her head away. She was afraid of what he might see, what she might reveal at that moment of vulnerability. But she was helpless to turn away from the demand of his gaze.

His look holding hers, Nick let his hips sink against hers. Her eyes widened endlessly as her body accepted his. She'd thought she'd forgotten but she discovered the memories were there. This was how it had always been, should have been forever. There was no past, no future, only Nick and the feel of his body above her, within her. This was what it was to feel complete.

Her fingers dug into the hard muscles of his hips as she pulled him to her, arching her back to take him deeper. It had been so long, she thought feverishly. He withdrew and then filled her again. The breath that exploded from her was half a sob. God, she'd forgotten how it felt, forgotten how he filled her, body and soul.

Her eyelids fell shut as she pressed the back of her head into the pillow, her heels digging into the bed as she sought to take him still farther into herself, so deep that nothing could ever separate them.

Nick groaned and lowered his body to hers, sliding his arms under her back and hooking his hands over her shoulders, holding her for the driving thrusts of his body. She met him, matching her movements to his, her breath coming in sobbing little pants that added to his arousal.

Tess could feel the burning pleasure building up inside her, could feel her skin flush with it. She was so close. Completion hovered just beyond her fingertips, drifting out of reach as the pleasure built and built until she was sure she would shatter into a million pieces.

And then she did shatter. And found what she'd sought.

She cried out, her body arching against Nick's, her fingers digging into the sweat-dampened muscles in his back. Nick felt the trembling convulsions that rippled over her and ground his teeth against the urge to follow her. He didn't want it to end. Not now. Not ever. But then her delicate contractions took him, caressing him, sending him tumbling headlong into pleasure.

Tess heard his guttural groan and tightened her arms around him, holding him, letting the powerful pulse of his climax carry her still higher.

For the first time in five years, she was whole, the emptiness in her soul filled.

IT WAS SEVERAL MINUTES before Nick found the energy to move. Several minutes after that before either of them spoke.

"Are you all right?"

All right? Lying with her head on his shoulder, his arms cradling her, Tess thought "all right" hardly captured how she felt. But she nodded without lifting her head from his shoulder. "I'm fine."

Except for the fact that reality was trying to intrude, reminding her this was a moment out of time, a slice of pretend before real life continued. A real life that didn't include Nick anymore.

Frowning, she pushed the thought away and shifted closer to him, easing her leg across his thighs. She'd only intended to cuddle close enough to keep the future at bay. But when she felt the solid pressure of him against her thigh, she was caught off guard by an answering response in the pit of her belly.

She moved her leg again and Nick groaned. Catching her around the waist, he slid her over him until she straddled his hips. Lifting herself, she took him inside, their soft moans echoing in the quiet room.

Reality—and the future—could be ignored for at least a little while longer.

Chapter Three

It felt so natural to wake in Nick's arms, so completely right, that it took Tess several minutes to start wondering what she was doing there. Opening her eyes, she found her field of vision filled by a muscled expanse of chest. Nick lay on his side, facing her, her head on his arm, his forearm resting in the curve of her waist.

For a moment, it was almost as if the last five years had never happened. She could pretend the divorce had been nothing but a bad dream. If she didn't look at the sleek, modern room, it might have been the bed they'd shared in the house they'd worked so hard to turn into a home.

She turned a deaf ear to the little voice that tried to point out that the last five years *had* happened and that this *wasn't* their old room. Just a little while longer, she pleaded with her conscience. Just a little more time to pretend. Last night had been wonderful. Magical. She didn't want to give up that magic just yet.

"Good morning." Nick's voice was sleep rough, the huskiness stroking over Tess's skin like a warm cloth. She'd been so absorbed in inner argument that she hadn't noticed when he opened his eyes.

"Good morning." She wondered if there was some protocol on how to behave when one found oneself in bed with one's ex-husband.

"I thought I'd dreamed you but you feel pretty real." She felt her cheeks flush at the look of sleepy hunger in Nick's eyes.

"I do?" At the moment, nothing about this situation felt real. And she wanted to keep it that way for just a little while longer.

"Very real." Nick's hand flattened against her lower back, shifting her closer. He took her mouth in a slow, thorough kiss. There was none of last night's urgency in this morning's embrace. Yet Tess found herself trembling, her skin almost painfully sensitized to his touch as his hand moved downward to flatten against her bottom and crush her gently to him. Feeling his arousal, Tess moaned softly against his mouth, her fingers flexing on his chest.

It was just the way she remembered it, she thought dimly. How many mornings had they awakened just this way? It didn't matter that they'd made love several times the night before, the hunger between them was always there, needing only a touch to turn a spark into fire.

This morning, it was a slow burn. Long, stroking touches, and soft whispers. There was an unspoken but mutual need to make it last forever. The completion was, if anything, more powerful for the leisurely climb to reach it. Tess arched into Nick's body as wave after wave of sensation rolled over her. Nick shuddered in her arms, his big body taut and hard as fulfillment took him.

He collapsed against her, a welcome weight on her trembling body. Tess held him, feeling tears burn the backs of her eyes. It had been so long since she'd felt this complete, this sense of wholeness. For five years she'd been telling herself she'd made her peace with her failed marriage, with her life without Nick. It had taken less than twelve hours to show her how wrong she'd been.

Nick started to shift to the side and Tess tightened her hold on him, suddenly afraid.

"I'm too heavy, honey," Nick murmured, forcing her to loosen her arms enough to allow him to roll from her. His arm slid under her, immediately pulling her to his side, but the closeness was not enough to reassure Tess. She closed her eyes, pushing back the fear.

"I've missed you, Tess." Nick's husky admission brought tears to her eyes and she blinked them back, pressing her cheek against his chest, savoring the way the matted hair felt against her skin.

"I've spent five years convincing myself it wasn't as good between us as I'd remembered." Nick's fingers sifted through the heavy black cape of her hair, arranging it so that it draped over her bare shoulder and onto his flat stomach. "I think I always knew I was lying to myself."

Tess said nothing. She wasn't sure she could force her voice out past the lump in her throat. It felt so wonderfully, terribly right to lie here in Nick's bed, in his arms. This wasn't the way it should be, she thought. It shouldn't feel like coming home to be here, like this, with her ex-husband.

"We need to talk, Tess."

The words sent a bolt of pure panic through her. She wasn't ready to talk about what had happened. She didn't even understand what had happened. The last thing she wanted to do was talk about it. Not until she felt a little less like she was standing on shifting ground.

"Not now."

"We can't put it off forever." His tone was gentle but implacable.

"I know." She tilted her head to smile up at him, hoping the morning light that filtered through the heavy black drapes was dim enough to conceal the panic that must be visible in her eyes. "But we don't have to talk right this minute, do we?"

"Why not?"

Because I'm scared to death of what you're going to say. Of what I might say. It's all happened too fast, Nick. I need time, time to figure out what I've done. And why.

"Because I'm starving," she told him apologetically.

"You're hungry?" Nick seemed surprised, as if he hadn't been expecting such a prosaic response.

"It's been a long time since Fran's party." His eyes searched her face, as if seeking some sign that she was being less than truthful. "You don't plan on starving me, do you?" she asked, thrusting out her lower lip in the merest hint of a pout.

The doubt vanished from Nick's expression and his mouth curved in a grin that went straight to her heart—her damned, traitorous heart.

"I suppose I could be persuaded to feed you." He frowned, thinking. "I don't have anything here, though. I cleaned the kitchen out before I went to Virginia last month. We'll have to go out."

"That's okay." Tess tried not to sound too eager. Out. That was exactly where she wanted to be. Out of this bed, out of this apartment, somewhere nice and neutral. Someplace where she could gather her thoughts without feeling as if she was surrounded by Nick.

"Okay." It was obvious that Nick didn't share her feelings, but since there was no food in the house, he couldn't argue. "The bathroom's through there." He nodded to a lacquered door opposite. "I'll shower down the hall. I'd suggest saving water and showering with a friend but I have a feeling you wouldn't get fed today."

Tess flushed and bit the inside of her lip to hold back the words that would have had them sharing a shower—and would have put off talking about what had happened between them. Nick seemed to be waiting for something but when she said nothing, he sighed and eased his arm out from under her before swinging his legs over the side of the bed and sitting up. He cast a last look over his shoulder at her slender body and stood up.

Tess felt her breath catch at the sheer, male beauty of him. Broad shoulders tapered to a narrow waist and sleek hips. He'd always worked out, getting up at dawn to run, going to the gym at lunch. With Nick, it was less a matter of vanity than it was a desire to feel his best. He'd always claimed that he was basically one of the laziest people in the world, he just worked hard to conceal it.

She watched him cross to the door with long, lazy strides. Her mouth was suddenly dry and she wondered at her own sanity. How could she let him out of her sight?

Nick turned at the door and caught her staring. Her expression must have revealed something of her thoughts because his smile was pure, masculine satisfaction, his eyes gleaming.

"Don't take forever in the shower, like you usually do. Anything over thirty minutes and I'm coming in after you." Grinning, he turned and disappeared into the hall. A moment later, Tess heard a door close.

Don't take forever in the shower, like you usually do.

Just as if they'd been sharing a house, as if the past five years had never happened.

Shivering, Tess closed her eyes. It wasn't that easy. It couldn't be. They weren't married anymore. And that had been largely her choice. She couldn't just fall back into the same old patterns. She couldn't just let five years of her life disappear as if they'd never happened. She drew a deep breath, inhaling the warm fragrance of Nick, the musky scent of their lovemaking.

She opened her eyes and looked at the sleek, modern decor, reminding herself that the last five years had really happened. This wasn't the cozy bedroom she and Nick had shared in the house they'd worked to restore. She was no longer a girl of twenty. She was a woman of twenty-five. A woman who was running a successful business of her own. She'd worked hard for that success, worked hard to convince herself that she was capable of having a life without Nick.

And last night, she'd walked—eyes wide open—into Nick's arms, into his bed. She heard the sound of water running and knew Nick must be showering. No doubt he assumed that she was doing the same. And that, when he came out, they'd go somewhere for breakfast and discuss... Discuss what? What did he think they needed to talk about?

Shivering, Tess slid off the bed and gathered up her clothing. There wasn't much, just her panties and her dress. Next time she went to a party where she was going to see her ex-husband, she was going to wear a great deal more clothing, she told herself, so distraught that the vow seemed sensible.

She darted into the bathroom and splashed water on her face, trying not to look at her reflection as she scrambled into her clothes. Her fingers patted ineffectually at her tangled hair. There was a comb in her purse. She'd worry about her hair when she'd reached the marginal safety of her car.

Because she wasn't going to wait for Nick to get out of the shower. She didn't know what he wanted to say, but she knew she wasn't up to hearing it. Not now. Not until she could figure out how she felt about last night. About him.

Tess crept across the bedroom with all the caution of a sneak thief and as much guilt. Since the water was still running, she felt reasonably safe, but there was no sense in taking chances. Once in the hallway, she ran across the living room, pausing just long enough to grab her shoes and purse.

At the door, she threw a last look over her shoulder, torn between the instinct that screamed at her to get while the getting was good and the deep, visceral urge to run back to the bedroom, back to Nick. With a muffled sob, she wrenched open the door and dashed out into the warm summer sunshine.

HE WASN'T GOING TO RUSH her this time. He would give her all the time she could possibly want. More even. Nick frowned at the tiled wall, letting the hot water sluice over his body as he repeated the vows to himself. He had another chance with Tess, a chance he hadn't even realized he wanted. But he had it and he wanted it and he wasn't going to blow it.

He shut the shower off and pushed open the glass door of the cubicle. He dried himself with a thick, blue towel. In this bathroom and the guest room, a soft colonial blue replaced the black-and-gray that accented the rest of the condo. When he'd bought the place, he'd been glad that the decorating was so diametrically opposed to the cozy, country Victorian look of the house he'd shared with Tess. But this morning, the black and gray, lacquer and leather all looked hard and cold and slightly pretentious.

Wrapping one towel around his hips, he rubbed a second one over his hair with a vigor that reflected his inner tension more than his desire for dry hair. This time was going to be different. This time, he was going to give her room. Time. In that last, awful conversation when Tess had told him she wanted a divorce, she'd said she felt as if she was suffocating in his shadow, that she wasn't even a person anymore, only his wife.

Nick frowned at his blurred reflection in the steamed-over mirror. He was sure it would never win him any awards for non-sexist thinking, but his first reaction had been to question why being his wife wasn't enough. His mother had always been happy being his father's wife. Before he could think better of it, he'd said as much, and he'd seen something die in Tess's eyes. Hope, perhaps?

He'd had five years to consider her words. He still didn't entirely understand what she'd meant. After all, he'd never asked her to stay home, never believed that a woman's place was strictly in the home. If she'd wanted something more, something like this shop she'd started, no one would have been more supportive than he. But Tess obviously hadn't believed that and that was one of the things that was going to have to change.

He was going to have to show her that he wasn't the chauvinist she imagined, that he could be as enlightened and supportive as the next man—or woman. And he wasn't going to rush her. They were going to start out by having a nice, quiet breakfast together, talking about what had happened, talking about the future. All nice and civilized.

And he was going to resist the urge to kidnap her and take her to Las Vegas and make her his wife before midnight. He could wait until at least noon tomorrow.

A rueful smile acknowledged that patience was not one of his strong suits. Especially not when it came to something he wanted as badly as he wanted Tess. But he wanted to keep her this time, and that meant doing things her way.

Looking more determined than patient, Nick left the bathroom and walked down the hall to his bedroom. It was empty, the rumpled covers silent witness to what had gone on there the night before. Cocking his head, Nick listened for the sound of the shower. He grinned when he heard only silence. Tess must be really hungry if she'd managed to take a shower in less than twenty minutes.

Opening the closet door, he pulled out a pair of jeans and a shirt. Tossing them on the tousled sheets, he got briefs from the dresser and stepped into them. By the time he had tugged the jeans over his hips and was buttoning them, it had begun to sink in that there was no noise coming from the bathroom.

Leaving the last button undone, Nick moved over to the black door and tapped lightly.

"Tess? Are you all right?"

There was no response. He stared at the sleek door for the space of several heartbeats, feeling a sudden tightness in his chest. He was almost surprised to see that his hand was steady as he reached out and pushed the door open.

The room was empty, the shiny black tile dry. The only sign that Tess had used the room at all was the fact that one towel had been draped crookedly over the rack.

His face expressionless, Nick turned and crossed the bedroom, going into the hall. It wasn't really necessary but he searched the entire condo, even looking in the utility room off the kitchen and stepping onto the balcony as if Tess might be hiding behind one of the potted plants. The way she'd been hiding behind that damned tree last night at the McKenzies'.

Nick's hands clenched over the balcony railing. The view that had sparkled with magic last night was gray and tired this morning. The classic Los Angeles mixture of haze and smog obscured the city.

She was gone.

He couldn't quite make the thought sink in. Any more than he'd been able to make it sink in when she'd told him she wanted a divorce. The comparison brought a wave of anger so fierce, he could feel his hands start to tremble. Spinning away from the rail, Nick strode into the living room. Without thinking, he swept through the condo again, as if he had to confirm that Tess was really gone.

He ended his search in the bedroom, standing in the middle of the floor, his fingers curled into fists at his sides, his eyes brilliant green with anger. She was gone, leaving nothing to show for her presence but a cup of cold coffee in the living room and the love-rumpled sheets.

With an inarticulate sound that was nearly a growl, he bent and ripped the sheets from the mattress. Carrying them through the living room and into the kitchen, he stuffed them in the trash, jamming them down until they were crushed into the container and then letting the lid bang down with a metallic clang.

Stepping back, his breath coming too quickly, he stared at the square black container. But he couldn't throw the memories away with the sheets.

Tess's eyes when she'd turned to look at him at the party last night. The feel of her skin under his hands, the way it heated at his touch, until she almost seemed to be melting into him.

"Not this time, Tess," he said aloud. "Not this time."

Spinning on one heel, he stalked out of the kitchen. Entering the bedroom again, he found the shirt he'd gotten out earlier lying on the floor.

Yanking it over his head, he picked up the trousers he'd discarded the night before, emptying the pockets with quick efficiency and stuffing wallet, cash and car keys into the pockets of his jeans. The rental car was still at the McKenzies' but it was just going to have to wait.

When the phone rang a third time, he cursed but moved to answer it. Snatching the receiver off the hook, he barked a hello into it.

"Nick?" A small voice sounded in his ear, shaken and on the verge of tears.

"Sara?" At her tone, he felt his anger toward Tess quickly drain, replaced by concern for his sister. "What's wrong?" he asked. "Are you all right?"

"It's... it's Dad," she said on a sob. "He's had a heart attack... and it doesn't look good."

No, it couldn't be. Bill Masters was as tough as they came. Nick's words reassured Sara as he tried to reassure himself with his thoughts. Their father was only sixty, he said, still young enough to recover from something like this.

"Don't worry, Sara. I'm leaving right now."

But by the time he set the receiver down, Nick was aware that his hand was not quite steady. His father was in the hospital. Possibly dying. It was inconceivable. Bill Masters was built like an oak tree and twice as strong.

He turned away from the phone, thrusting his fingers through his damp hair, destroying the dubious order it had held. His eyes lit on the stripped bed, and he closed them. He couldn't bear the sight of it.

Tess.

He couldn't go after her now. That was going to have to wait. *He* was going to have to wait. He'd waited five years for an explanation. He supposed another day or two wouldn't really matter.

But now or a week from now, he was going to have an explanation.

Chapter Four

"The shipment from Crafthouse got here Friday. The kits are on the wall across from the register." Tess glanced up from her clipboard to make sure her companion had heard her.

"Just at child height, I suppose." Josie lifted her eyes from the skein of floss she was untangling, the result of a bored four-year-old's inquisitive fingers.

"They're sealed in plastic," Tess offered soothingly.

"It won't matter." Josie refused to be soothed. The gloomy expression sat oddly on her round features. "The little darlings will find a way to destroy them."

"You're just upset because Mrs. Levine's grandchildren got into the floss drawers last week."

"Mrs. Levine's grandchildren should only be allowed out on a leash."

Tess grinned but didn't comment. Dealing with a customer's ill-behaved offspring was just one of the things a retailer had to deal with. Despite her grumpy expression, Josie coped better than most. Tess made a note on the clipboard before setting it on the overcrowded desk that was wedged into the tiny room she somewhat grandiloquently called her office. It was as much a storeroom as it was an office, the walls lined with boxes of floss and needlework kits awaiting their turn on the shelves and racks in the front of the store.

She'd started the shop with money obtained by mortgaging the Victorian Nick had insisted she take in the divorce settlement. Friends had told her she was crazy to risk her house. Didn't she know the statistics about how many small businesses failed in the first year? And a needlework shop? What kind of business was that?

But Needles & Pins hadn't failed. It had prospered. This year, for the first time, Tess was going to be able to take out not only living expenses, but enough to start putting money in the bank. And it was a good thing, too, she thought. This year she was going to need it. She sighed and reached for her cup of herbal tea.

Josie worked the last knot loose from the floss and began winding the bright green thread around her hand. It couldn't be sold, of course, but one of them was sure to find a use for it in their own needlework projects.

Tess cradled the teacup between her hands and told herself that she had too much to do to be sitting here doing absolutely nothing. She should tackle some of the paperwork that was covering her desk. She should prepare for the Christmas rush that was sure to descend on them now that it was late November. Or she could go out and make sure everything was ready for the shop to open in twenty minutes. But she didn't move. It felt good to just sit here, watching Josie start on another tangled skein, and thinking about nothing in particular.

"I suppose I should get up and go dust the counter or something." Since she hadn't bothered to take her feet off the box on which they were propped, Tess's comment was clearly an idle threat.

"I'll dust the counter." Josie busily worked another knot loose. "You should stay off your feet."

"I'm all but over the cold," Tess said.

"It's not the cold I'm worried about," Josie said, giving her friend a stern look from under her pale lashes.

"I'm fine." Tess swung her feet to the floor and stood up to prove it.

"Have you heard from Nick?"

The question caught Tess off guard, causing a sharp little ache in her chest.

"There's no reason I should," she said, proud to hear that her voice was level.

"Hah." Josie's snort was eloquent if not particularly polite. "He's a jerk."

"No, he's not. What happened between us was as much my doing as it was his. Maybe he thinks I should be the one to call him."

"Well, you should." Josie didn't seem to think there was anything odd in her abrupt about-face. She rested her hands on the table and tilted her head to fix Tess with a stern look. "You should have called him months ago."

"We've gone over this before." Tess's thinning patience was audible. "I'm not going to call Nick. We slept together. It happens all the time between ex-husbands and wives. It was just one of those things."

She shrugged to show how completely she'd put the incident behind her. She could only hope the older woman couldn't see the effort that casual gesture took.

"If you think I believe that it meant nothing to you, then you must think I'm a whole lot stupider than I look. I saw the way you watched the phone and I know how much you want to tell Nick—"

"Enough." Tess's sharp tone cut Josie off in midstream. She drew a deep breath and continued more quietly. "I don't want to talk about it anymore, Josie. I've made my decision, and obviously Nick has made his. It was just a stupid encounter and it's over." She lifted her hand when Josie drew breath to interrupt. "I don't want to hear another word about it."

Josie's mouth shut with a snap, her soft chin set with annoyance. Seeing that she'd made her point, Tess drew a relieved breath. Not that she was foolish enough to think that it was the last she'd hear on the subject. A romantic to the core, Josie simply couldn't believe that everybody didn't get the sort of happy ending she felt they should have.

Tess wished now that she hadn't told Josie what had happened that night. But she'd needed someone to talk to and Josie was not just her employee, but her best friend. But for the last three months, she'd put up with more lectures than she could count.

"I'm going to make sure everything is in order," Tess said again, forcing the lingering irritation from her voice.

"Just don't overdo it." Her concern made Tess feel guilty for snapping at her.

"I run a needlework shop. I'm not a stevedore. I don't think lifting a few skeins of yarn is going to do any harm."

"As long as that's all you lift," Josie warned her.

"Yes, Mother. If anyone asks for more than two skeins of yarn at a time, I'll call you."

"See that you do," Josie said calmly.

"I'm going to go unlock the front door, if you don't think that'll be overdoing it," Tess said with heavy sarcasm.

Josie appeared to consider and then nodded, setting her sandy hair swinging. "I think that should be all right."

"Remind me to fire you after Christmas."

"I'll make a note of it."

Tess was shaking her head as she left the tiny office. There were certainly advantages to being friends with someone who worked for you. But there were also disadvantages, like Josie's tendency to fuss over her like a mother hen. Still, there was something rather sweet about the concern.

Without Josie's friendship, her life would be a lot emptier.

Her eyes skimmed the crowded walls as she moved through the store. Even after four years, it still amazed her to look at the shop and know that it was hers. Something she'd built with her own drive and hard work. No matter what other mistakes she made, *this* was something she'd done right.

She slid the key in the front door lock but she didn't turn it immediately. She looked out at the sunshine pouring over the sidewalk just beyond the blue-and-white striped awning that shielded the front windows. This morning, the weatherman had cheerfully announced that it was going to be seventy-five degrees and sunny today, with the same for the foreseeable future. It was hard to believe it was barely four weeks until Christmas.

She sighed and twisted the key in the lock, officially opening the shop for the day. Lingering by the window, she tried to imagine the street outside covered in snow, but the brightly colored poppies blooming in the flower beds that lined the sidewalk made the image difficult to capture.

The holidays were her least favorite time of year. And the Southern California sunshine didn't make her like them any more. She remembered her parents, both now gone. Her father had been career army and he'd always been eager for any transfer that might advance his career. Since he was also a difficult man to get along with, his superior officers had had no hesitation about transferring him as often as he liked.

He'd simply come home and tell Tess and her mother to start packing. They were on the road again. They'd seldom lived in one place for more than a year. And for Tess, a little girl who didn't make friends easily, the holidays had generally served to emphasize her loneliness, and she had learned to endure rather than enjoy them.

Until she met Nick.

Her mouth curved in a half smile, remembering that first Christmas with him. Her first Christmas as his wife, though just barely. They'd been married on Christmas Eve in a tiny chapel in Burbank. Nick had paid an outrageous fee to convince the woman to marry them, insisting they had to spend their first Christmas together as husband and wife. The first of many, he'd said.

Only it hadn't been. Tess's smile faded. They'd only had one more holiday together. But those two Christmases stood out in her memory as the only times she'd really understood the holiday spirit. Since then, the memories had become just one more regret to haunt her during the last few weeks of the year. And this year, there was more reason than ever for regrets.

Though she'd been staring out the window, she was so wrapped up in her thoughts that when the bell over the door rang, announcing the day's first customer, she was startled.

"I need another skein of Christmas red floss," the woman announced as soon as she saw Tess. Her tone hovered on the edge of panic and Tess gave her a soothing smile.

"Do you have the color number?" she asked, as she led the way to the oak cabinet that held the floss.

Ten minutes later, the bell jingled again as the door closed behind the woman. She'd left in a calmer state than she arrived, the floss tucked carefully in her purse. Tess felt her melancholy mood lift. There was something very satisfying about being able to give a customer just what she wanted, even when it was something as simple as a skein of floss.

She had to stop dwelling on the past, she reminded herself as she dusted the cash register keys unnecessarily. Whether it was her marriage or the night she'd spent with Nick after Fran McKenzie's party. Both were over and done and if she'd been so foolish as to think that night might have meant something to Nick, then his silence over the last few months had told her just how wrong she was.

You were the one who ran out on him.

Yes, but he could have called.

Why should he? Maybe he thought this was the way you wanted it. A one-night stand. No entanglements. No regrets.

He knows me better than that. Doesn't he?

Tess frowned at the Christmas kits that hung on the wall opposite the register. *Did* Nick know her better than that?

"Why don't I handle things out front this morning?" Josie's words preceded her. Tess blinked and forced her thoughts into focus on the present, pushing aside unanswerable questions about the past.

"Okay." She moved out from behind the glass-fronted desk. "I've got a bunch of paperwork to catch up on."

She retreated to her office and shut the door. Despite the clutter, the little room had become a sort of haven since she opened the shop. Here, she was surrounded by the evidence of what she'd accomplished. There were no old memories to disturb her. Except that lately, the memories seemed to follow her wherever she went.

"It's just that it's Christmas," she muttered, frowning at the row of brightly colored cards Josie had hung on a string draped over the door.

And it had been three months since Fran's party—and still not a word from Nick. But she wasn't going to think about that, she reminded herself briskly. The future was what was important and she had plenty of reason to look forward rather than back. From now on the past was going to stay where it belonged—in the past.

And she might as well start by keeping busy. She tilted her head as she heard the soft jingle of the front door. Maybe waiting on customers was just what she needed today. The paperwork could wait. Distraction was what she needed now.

She walked out of the office, a friendly smile firmly in place. The past she'd just decided to forget was standing in her shop.

"Nick."

His name was hardly more than a breath. He couldn't possibly have heard her. Yet his eyes slid past Josie, focusing on Tess's frozen figure. Tess felt the impact of that look all the way to her toes.

It wasn't possible that he was here, in her shop. Yet there he stood, the light catching in the heavy gold of his hair, his vivid green eyes locked on her.

Tess felt a wild tangle of emotions. She was trembling with relief—he hadn't forgotten, hadn't simply let her vanish from his life. She was furious—what had taken him so long? She was resentful—how dare he intrude on the one place that wasn't already filled with memories of him? And there was that odd little clench of hunger in the pit of her stomach—the one she always felt when she saw Nick. That never changed. Until the day she died, she knew she'd feel that same hunger, that same need.

"Tess."

The sound of her name released her frozen limbs, making it possible for her to step forward.

"Nick. What a surprise." If the greeting fell short of the casual tone she'd have liked, at least her voice was steady. The same could not be said of her fingers. She slipped her hands into the pockets of her floral cotton jumper and summoned what she hoped was a Mona Lisa-like smile. "What brings you to this neighborhood?"

"I wanted to see you."

"Oh, really?" Tess stopped at the end of the counter and leaned unobtrusively against it, half-afraid that her knees might betray her and deposit her unceremoniously on the floor at his feet. "What for?"

"I think we should talk." Nick glanced at Josie, who was making no secret of her interest in the conversation, her eyes going from Nick to Tess as if she were watching a tennis match.

"About what?" Couldn't she manage something more than a two-word sentence?

"About us," he said bluntly and Tess leaned more heavily against the counter, feeling her knees start to tremble.

"Us?" she managed. God, now she was reduced to one-word sentences. What did he mean by "us?" They'd ceased to be "us" five years ago.

Hadn't they?

NICK WATCHED COLOR flood her cheeks and then recede, leaving her skin the color of pale porcelain. He'd intended to approach things more subtly: start a light conversation, ask about the shop, then move on from there. But his first glimpse of Tess had brought such a welter of emotion roiling up inside him that he'd found himself incapable of anything but the most direct approach.

He wanted to snatch her into his arms and kiss her senseless. He wanted to grab her and shake her for walking out on him—again. And he wanted to just hold her and feel her against him, where she belonged.

“I’m not sure there’s anything to talk about,” Tess said at last, her voice thin and uncertain.

“I disagree. I think we have a great deal to talk about.” Nick didn’t bother to disguise the iron hand beneath the polite tone. He’d had three months to think about this meeting and the time had done nothing to soften his determination to understand why she’d run away from him—again.

“I can’t really spare the time, Nick.” Tess turned and began busily straightening the magazine rack at her elbow. “I have a shop to run. Christmas is a very busy time.”

“You could spare a few minutes for a cup of coffee, couldn’t you?” The words were a question but the tone was a demand and he didn’t care who heard it, whether it was Tess or the middle-aged woman who was watching their exchange with open interest. He and Tess were going to talk. And if he had to come back every day for the next year, that’s what he’d do.

“I have a lot to do,” Tess said. “This is a busy time of year for retailers, you know.”

“So I see.” Nick glanced pointedly around the shop, empty but for the three of them. Tess flushed and set her chin.

“I have a great deal of paperwork to do. I can’t just run off anytime I want.”

"The papers aren't going to go anywhere," Josie commented, to no one in particular. "You've been putting them off for a week now. A couple more hours won't matter."

"I've already put them off long enough," Tess said, giving Josie a warning look.

"I can take care of things out here." Josie ignored the warning.

"Thank you." Nick turned the full force of his smile on her and Tess was unsurprised to see Josie blink, looking as dazed as a deer caught in a car's headlights.

IT WOULD SERVE HER right if Nick broke her heart, too, Tess thought, with unaccustomed malice. What kind of a friend was she, anyway? It was obvious to everyone that she didn't want to go anywhere with her ex-husband. The odd trembly feeling in her stomach was annoyance, not excitement. Just because she'd spent the last three months wondering why he hadn't tried to see her, it didn't mean that she'd *wanted* to see him. If he turned and walked out the door right now, it would be fine with her.

Liar. Her conscience nudged her sharply. The fact was, just being in the same room with Nick made her feel alive in a way she hadn't felt in months—three months, to be exact. And even if he hadn't had the ability to make her feel tinglingly alive, there were still plenty of reasons why she should talk to him.

"I guess the place won't fall apart if I'm not around for an hour," she said, trying to sound as if she weren't being railroaded into a decision.

"Of course it won't," Josie said, her tone so hearty that Tess wanted to hit her. "We won't start getting really busy till mid-afternoon," she added, directing the comment to Nick, as if giving him permission to keep Tess until then.

"I'll certainly be back long before that," Tess said quickly, cutting off any reply Nick might have made. They were just going to go have a quick cup of coffee and settle a few things. The last thing she wanted was to spend the afternoon with her ex-husband.

And if she repeated that a few hundred times, she might come to believe it.

Chapter Five

At Tess's suggestion, they walked down the street to the small Fifties-style café that had opened a few months ago and had been doing a brisk business ever since. Walking next to Nick, Tess was vividly aware of the sheer size of him. At six foot two, Nick loomed over her own height of five foot nothing. She found herself wishing she were wearing three-inch heels instead of the comfortable flats she had on. But she knew it would take more than high heels to make her feel on an equal footing with her ex-husband.

Nick held the door for her when they arrived at the café and Tess murmured her thanks as she entered. She caught a faint whiff of his after-shave as she brushed by him. The familiar scent brought an equally familiar response—a little flutter in her stomach, a slightly breathless feeling that she well remembered. It had been that same breathless feeling that had made her ignore her common sense three months ago.

She couldn't do this, she thought. She couldn't sit across a table from Nick and calmly discuss their relationship. She hadn't been able to do it five years ago, or for that matter three months ago, and nothing had changed.

She was hovering on the edge of full-blown panic when she felt Nick move up behind her. In a ridiculous about-face, she immediately felt reassured by his presence. He'd always done that—made her feel safe and secure, made it seem as if he could take care of any problem that might crop up. Even when he *was* the problem.

She bit back a slightly hysterical giggle. *I'm losing my mind,* she thought. That was the only possible explanation for the way her mood was seesawing between panic and excitement, between wanting to run from Nick and wanting to cling to him. Insanity was the obvious answer. At least, it was the only answer she wanted to consider at the moment.

IT WAS TOO LATE for breakfast and too early for lunch and the café was nearly empty. The waitress, clad in bobby socks and a pink poodle skirt, showed them to a red vinyl booth. There was a box next to the window for selecting songs to be played on the vintage jukebox near the counter, and bright plastic holders for the cone-shaped paper water cups the waitress filled for them.

"Two coffees," Nick told the girl, waving away the menus she was offering.

"Make mine a decaf," Tess said quickly.

"Since when are you drinking decaf?" he asked as the waitress left. "I thought you couldn't live without your daily doses of caffeine."

"I'm trying to cut back." She shrugged, dismissing the change.

He looked as if he might have pursued the topic, but the waitress reappeared promptly, setting a pair of thick white mugs on the table. Tess was grateful for the interruption, though she was sure anything he'd have said would have been nothing more than idle conversation. Lots of people decided to cut back on caffeine, she reminded herself.

Nick pushed the cream pitcher toward her automatically and reached for the sugar for himself. Watching him pour two heaping spoonfuls of sugar into his cup, Tess felt the backs of her eyelids sting. Nick's love of sweets had always seemed an endearing trait, a touch of boyishness that had made him a little less intimidating. She lowered her eyes to her cup, not wanting to remember the other things she'd found endearing about him.

NICK FELT THE SILENCE stretching and found his mind suddenly gone blank. He'd had three months to think of all the things he wanted to say to Tess, all the questions he wanted to ask. Clever phrases had tripped through his thoughts. But now that he had Tess in front of him, more or less a captive audience, they showed no sign of tripping from his lips.

He stared at the swags of plastic holly that decorated the edges of the booth. The red ribbon bows that adorned it had a vaguely disarrayed look to them, as if they'd seen one too many holiday seasons.

Christmas. It hardly seemed possible that it was less than a month away. Last week's Thanksgiving celebration should have been a clue, he supposed. But it still hadn't prepared him for the holiday now rushing toward him.

And still the silence stretched.

Nick slid his eyes back to Tess. She was staring intently out the window, as if fascinated by the traffic in the street. He allowed his gaze to linger. She looked as good as he remembered—better even.

Her hair was pulled back from her face and caught at the nape of her neck with a big bow. The bow was the same soft blue as the cotton shirt she wore under her loose jumper. There was something slightly girlish about the outfit, but the curve of her mouth and the outlines of her figure were all woman.

He shifted uncomfortably in the booth and looked away from her. Answers. That was what he was here for. It wouldn't do to let himself get distracted by noticing how beautiful she was. Heaven knew, she was beautiful enough to distract a saint, which he was far from being, but he had to remember why he was here. So he plunged in without preamble.

"Why did you run off without a word?"

THE SUDDEN QUESTION made Tess jump. She'd expected it, of course. She'd been expecting it for three months. And she still didn't know how to answer.

"I didn't think a postmortem was necessary," she said, knowing that it was neither the truth nor an answer that would satisfy him. But she couldn't even begin to explain the wave of panic that had sent her running from his bedroom. He'd never understand. She didn't understand it completely herself.

"Bull." The blunt rejection startled her. Her eyes jerked to his face.

"Excuse me?"

"You heard me." Nick leaned forward, pinning her to the booth with his gaze. "That's a bull excuse and you and I both know it."

"I don't know what you mean," Tess said. She twisted her coffee cup nervously between her hands. This conversation was not starting out at all the way she'd envisioned.

"It wasn't a postmortem you were afraid of, Tess. You weren't afraid of going over a relationship that was already dead. You were afraid we might find that there was still quite a bit of life in it. Which there obviously is or you wouldn't have been in my bed to start with."

"Sleeping with someone doesn't necessarily imply a commitment, Nick." Tess lowered her hands to her lap to conceal their trembling.

"It does for you. You forget how well I know you."

"*Knew* me, Nick. You *knew* me five years ago. I've changed."

"Not that much."

He looked so sure, so...male. Tess felt anger start to burn away her nervousness. How dare he wait three months to contact her and then sit there looking so smug? So full of answers about how she'd felt, what she'd thought?

"I could have had several lovers since the divorce."

"But you didn't. In fact, I'd be willing to bet that you haven't had *any* lovers since we broke up."

"What makes you so sure?" she snapped. Her fingers curled into palms that tingled with the urge to smack the confidence from his annoyingly handsome face.

"Because it was like making love to a virgin again." Nick leaned toward her, his voice low and intimate. "And I know exactly how that felt. Remember, Tess?"

Remember? Tess felt her face flame. As if she could possibly forget that he'd been her first lover, her *only* lover, damn him. She wished she could throw half a dozen other men in his face.

"What's your point?" she asked, sidestepping his question.

"The point is that it was not a casual one-night stand for you."

Now how was she supposed to argue with that? She had no desire to claim she made a habit of one-night stands, even if he'd believe her, which he obviously wouldn't. On the other hand, she wasn't ready to admit to Nick that the night she'd spent with him three months ago had meant as much to her as it had. The man was arrogant enough as it was.

In the face of uncertainty, Tess settled for the one completely safe response. She shrugged. Nick drew in a quick breath as if her noncommittal response had annoyed him. She was slightly shocked by the pleasure that thought gave her. It was childish but she couldn't summon up any sincere regret.

"Tess, it wasn't a one-night stand for me, either," Nick said at last, his tone struggling for equanimity. "I've thought about you a lot since that night."

"And you've had *plenty* of time to think," Tess snapped. She immediately wished the words unspoken. The last thing she'd wanted to do was reveal how much his three months of silence had stung.

The flare of pleasure in Nick's eyes told her he knew exactly what her words meant. Cursing her quick tongue, she lifted her coffee cup and took a drink, trying to look indifferent.

"I started to come after you," Nick said, making it clear that her casual air fooled no one.

"Car trouble?" she asked sweetly, abandoning pretense.

"I was on my way out the door that morning when Sara called and told me that Dad had just had a heart attack."

"Oh, no!" The anger Tess had nursed for three months disappeared in an instant. "Oh, Nick, I didn't know. How is he?"

"He's going to make it. If the family can keep him from trying to work himself to death." Nick wondered if she was even aware of having reached across the table to touch the back of his hand. He turned his hand, closing his fingers over hers.

"He's very strong," she said reassuringly. "I can't imagine anything keeping him down for long."

"He was giving orders from his hospital bed," he said, smiling at the memory.

"I'm not surprised." Tess's smile was soft as she thought of her former father-in-law. It had always been easy to see where Nick had gotten his drive and determination. But Bill Masters had never made her feel as if she might be swallowed up in his shadow. Of course, maybe that was because she hadn't been head over heels in love with him.

"Dad was in the midst of several projects and I've spent the last three months keeping things on track and browbeating him into obeying his doctor's orders."

Which explained why he hadn't tried to see her before now. So all these months of hurt, of building anger—even when she'd known that anger wasn't quite fair—had been for no reason. The realization left Tess with a hollow feeling inside. She hadn't realized how much she'd been clinging to the anger and hurt. Or maybe what she'd really been doing was hiding behind it. But there was nothing to hide behind now and she felt as if she'd been stripped of a shield, leaving her exposed. Vulnerable.

"Did you think I was just ignoring what had happened?" Nick asked. He ran his thumb absently over the back of her hand, sending shivers of awareness down her spine. Tess hadn't even realized that he held her hand until that moment. The feel of his fingers around hers felt disturbingly right. Uneasily aware of a reluctance to do so, she drew her fingers from his and cupped them around her coffee cup.

"I didn't know." She shrugged. "You didn't call. I thought you might want to forget it had happened. Maybe that's what we both should have done."

"Do you hate seeing me so much that you'd rather I'd forgotten?" Nick's tone was completely neutral, denying her any hint of what he was thinking, giving no clue as to what her answer meant to him, if anything.

"I don't hate you," she said at last. "And I'm glad you didn't forget."

Now why had she added that? Why reveal that it mattered to her one way or another?

Because it was Nick and he mattered more than she wanted to admit, even to herself. He always had. And that night had only drawn the ties tighter. Of course, she didn't have to admit as much to him. Well, it was too late to take the words back. They probably didn't mean anything to him, anyway.

NICK HADN'T REALIZED how tautly he was holding himself until he heard Tess's words and felt the tension leave his shoulders. Over the past weeks, his time had been more than filled with trying to keep the business and his family on an even keel. There'd been little time for personal reflection. But in the back of his mind had been the knowledge that, as soon as he could manage to redistribute some of the responsibilities that had fallen his way, he was going to find Tess and get the explanation he wanted—needed.

Yet now, sitting across the table from her, he found himself less interested in explanations than in the way the light caught in her hair. He couldn't help but notice the tiny golden flecks that made her dark eyes so warm. Or the coral tint of her mouth. Was it just his overheated imagination or had she actually managed to grow even more beautiful in the last three months? There seemed to be a glow about her, an inner illumination he'd never noticed before.

He looked away, aware that he was becoming aroused. Worse than a teenager on a Friday night date, he thought in disgust. But then, Tess had always had the ability to do that to him, to make him lose his control in a way no other woman had ever done.

"The phone rings both ways, you know. Why didn't you call me?"

WHY HADN'T SHE CALLED him? There was no one answer to that question. The answers had changed as the weeks slid by. Tess's eyes slid to his and then away. She turned her coffee cup between her hands, focusing her gaze on the aimless motion, afraid of what Nick might read in her expression.

"I guess I should have," she said finally, when it became clear that he was waiting for her response.

"So, why didn't you?"

"I don't know." She lifted one shoulder in a half shrug and slanted a quick look at him. "I felt bad about running out like the heroine in a gothic novel fleeing a turreted mansion."

"I didn't even show you my turrets," Nick protested.

Tess smiled, grateful to him for trying to lighten the atmosphere. Her smile faded with his next question.

"Why did you run out, Tess?"

Another question to which she could only give half an answer. She couldn't possibly try to explain the tangled reasoning that had made running away seem like such an obvious choice. The waitress arrived just then to refill their cups, giving Tess a few seconds to consider the best answer.

When the woman had gone, Tess picked up the cream and poured some into her cup before lifting her spoon. Watching the pale swirl blend with the dark brew, she was aware of Nick's eyes on her, aware that she owed him the truth, even if it wasn't all the truth.

"Everything had moved so quickly." She set her spoon down and lifted her eyes to his face. "I hadn't expected to see you at Fran's. I hadn't thought of you in ages," she said bluntly. "If someone had asked me, I would have said I didn't feel anything but indifference toward you."

"Please, Tess, you'll make my head swell." Nick's ironic tone and pained expression drew a half smile from her.

"Sorry, but you wanted an answer." The lightness faded quickly, however. "It just happened so fast, Nick. One minute, you were part of my past. The next we were in bed together. And then you said we needed to talk."

"It seemed like a pretty obvious next step," Nick said.

"It was. Of course we needed to talk. But I didn't know what I was supposed to say and I was scared to death of what you might say."

"What did you *think* I was going to say?" he asked, frowning.

"I don't know." Tess looked away. She couldn't explain that she'd been afraid he would say he didn't want to see her again and equally terrified that he might suggest the opposite.

"It wasn't a logical reaction," she admitted. "It was emotional. I got dressed and left without thinking it out clearly, I guess. I panicked and acted like an idiot."

Nick didn't say anything for several seconds, letting the silence stretch while he considered her words. Tess took a sip of her coffee and glanced at the street outside, half-surprised to see the bright sunshine. This didn't seem like the kind of conversation that should be taking place in daylight. If this were a movie, the scene would have been a quiet table in an intimate café, perhaps with soft music playing in the background. It definitely would not be filmed with the two of them sitting in a red vinyl booth decorated with sagging holly swags, sunlight spilling in through the window beside them and Bobby Darin singing "Splish, Splash" as accompaniment. Which all went to prove that life didn't always imitate art, she supposed.

Tess lifted her coffee cup and took a drink. She felt oddly calm. Nick was right. They *had* needed to talk. The question was: Now that they'd straightened out some of the misunderstanding, where did they go from here? Now that Nick had the explanation he'd wanted, was that the end of it? Was he going to walk away with a polite handshake?

Could she let him walk away without telling him the whole truth?

Her conscience had been jabbing her for weeks and she'd silenced it by pointing to his obvious indifference. But it hadn't been indifference that had kept him away. What would she tell her conscience now?

"I have to admit that it's the first time I've been the cause of a panic attack," Nick said at last.

"It wasn't you, Nick. It was me. Everything happened so fast, there was no time to think. And when I had a few minutes to think, I panicked."

"Remind me not to leave you alone while I shower next time," he said lightly.

The implication that there might be a next time was enough to make Tess's mouth go dry. Her eyes dropped from his face to the speckled surface of the table. Did she want a next time? She shied away from the answer.

"Where do we go from here, Tess?" The quiet question brought her attention back to his face.

Why couldn't his eyes be a nice muddy color instead of clear, piercing green? How was a woman supposed to think intelligently with those eyes on her? How was she supposed to think intelligently when her pulse beat too quickly and all she could think about was the words next time?

"I don't know," she said slowly.

"Do you regret that night?"

Regret? It had changed her life forever, changed it in ways Nick knew nothing about. But did she regret it? Why did he keep asking her questions she didn't want to answer?

"I should."

HEARING THE TACIT admission, Nick had to suppress a smile. She might not be willing to say the words, but she didn't regret that night any more than he did. It wasn't much, but it was a start. He reached across the table and took her hand, holding it despite her automatic attempt to withdraw.

"Tess, I think we've both got to admit that there's still something between us." Startled blue eyes swept to his face and her fingers went still. She said nothing, and try as he might, Nick couldn't read her expression.

Setting his jaw, he continued, knowing that for his own peace of mind, the words had to be said. She could pitch him out of her life if she wanted, but he wasn't going without saying what he'd come to say.

"I want to see you again."

TESS'S HAND JUMPED in his, as if the flat statement had a physical impact. If her life had depended on it, she couldn't have looked away from him. She could only stare at him, frozen and silent with shock.

He wanted to see her again. Not once since he'd shown up this morning had she let that thought cross her mind.

She felt a tiny shiver run down her spine. She wished she could attribute it to cold winter weather, but not in Southern California. No, she had to be honest—with herself if no one else—and admit that the shiver was born of pure anticipation. To be seeing Nick again. Their brief courtship stood out in her memory as the happiest time of her life.

But he hadn't said anything about a courtship, she reminded herself.

"Why?"

If the blunt question surprised him, he didn't allow it to show.

"There's something between us, Tess. You can't deny it, even if you want to."

He paused, as if anticipating an argument, but she said nothing. There was more between them than even he knew.

"What happened between us that night of Fran's party made it pretty obvious that whatever caused you to ask me for a divorce five years ago, it didn't kill the attraction between us."

"There's more to a relationship than a physical attraction." Tess stirred restlessly against the vinyl booth. She tried to pull her hand from his, but Nick refused to allow it, his fingers tightening over hers.

"It's more than physical attraction, Tess, and we both know it."

"Maybe it's nothing more than nostalgia. We used to be married and a lot of the old feelings are still there," she suggested, knowing she'd be devastated if he accepted the glib explanation.

"Is that what you think it is?" Nick's eyes demanded nothing less than the truth.

"No," she whispered, shaking her head.

"Neither do I." He stroked his thumb absently over the back of her hand, the rhythmic gesture making it almost impossible for her to gather her thoughts into a coherent pattern. "I want to see you, Tess. No expectations, no promises. I just don't want to walk away from what we have. Whatever it is."

Tess hesitated, torn between a desperate need to say yes and the impulse to run. Yes, she wanted to see him. Yes, she wanted to find out what still lay between them. Almost equally strong was the old fear that she'd find herself swallowed up by his shadow, that Tess Armstrong would cease to exist, becoming nothing more than an unimportant extension of Nick Masters.

"We wouldn't rush things?" Her voice was hardly more than a whisper.

Sensing her surrender, Nick's fingers tightened over her hand.

"We'll take it as slow as you like," he promised.

It was such a risk, she thought. But there were more reasons to agree than even Nick knew about.

"No expectations?" As if her heart wasn't already swelling with expectation.

"Not a one."

"If it doesn't work out, no regrets?" Only over the death of a dream she hardly dared admit to having.

"No regrets."

"No sex?" Sleeping with him would only make it impossible to think clearly.

"No sex." Nick hesitated a moment over that one, his mouth twisting a little ruefully. "It's more than sex. I'll admit we're a pretty combustible combination, but there's more to it than that. You and I both know it."

She couldn't deny it but she didn't have to admit it, either, she thought, feeling a little defiant. Not that it would make a difference if she did. Nick would know she was lying.

"Are we agreed? We're going to see where this goes?"

"Agreed."

And heaven help her.

Chapter Six

"You're seeing *who* again!"

Nick winced as his youngest sister's voice rose perilously close to a shout, threatening both the health of his eardrums and the studied peacefulness of his decorous office at Masters Architectural. At that decibel level, soon every one of his employees would know about his love life.

"You heard me."

"I heard you but I can't believe I did." Hope fixed her brother with a look that held equal parts outrage and pleading. "Tell me you're not seeing Tess again."

"I'm not seeing Tess again," Nick parroted obediently.

"How could you, Nick? After the way she walked out on you five years ago." Hope's eyes, the same brilliant green as her brother's, were filled with reproach.

"You make it sound like she disappeared into the night, taking the family silver and my faithful hound with her."

Hope refused to be humored out of her mood. "That's practically what she did. Disappear into the night, I mean."

"Don't be dramatic, Hope. We had a perfectly civilized divorce." Nick leaned back against the supple leather of his desk chair and looked at his youngest, and though he rarely admitted as much, his most loved sister.

Of all his family, he knew Hope would be the toughest one to sell on the idea of him renewing old ties with his ex-wife. Not that he was doing that, at least not exactly. He wasn't ready to put a label on what was happening between him and Tess. Were they renewing old ties, making new ones or just wasting their time? All he knew was that, whatever had drawn them together in the first place, divorce and a five-year separation hadn't been strong enough to destroy.

"Now there's an interesting phrase: a civilized divorce. There was nothing civilized about it and you and I both know it."

"Well, it certainly wasn't *War of the Roses,*" Nick said.

"You can't tell me you weren't upset," she snapped.

"Of course I was upset. No one wants to watch their marriage break up." *Especially when you aren't quite sure just why it's breaking up,* he thought. But he wasn't going to say as much to Hope. It would probably just set her off again.

Tess and Hope were only a year apart in age and the moment he'd introduced the two of them, they'd hit it off. A friendship had developed that had little to do with the fact they were related by marriage. The relationship hadn't survived the divorce.

Hope, at twenty-one, had been completely unable to understand or to forgive what she saw as Tess's betrayal of Nick. He'd done his best to convince her that he and Tess getting a divorce didn't mean she had to sever her friendship with his soon-to-be ex-wife. But Hope hadn't been interested in his calm assurances. Maybe she'd sensed how rocky he was under the cool facade he'd assumed. Maybe she'd seen Tess's decision as a personal blow.

Whatever it had been, he'd known she wouldn't be thrilled at the thought of him seeing Tess again. On the other hand, she was his sister—his baby sister at that—and she was just going to have to learn to live with the idea.

"There's no sense in you getting in a snit, Hope." Nick stood up and came around his desk.

"What a chauvinist you are, Nick. I'm not in a snit. I'm concerned to see you doing something really dumb. You'd feel the same way if it were me." She eyed him without much favor as he sank onto the wide black leather sofa next to her.

"I'm your older brother. I'm supposed to be a chauvinist where you're concerned. It's part of the job description. You, on the other hand, are the younger sister." He reached out to tug a lock of her silky blond hair. "You are supposed to look up to me with admiring eyes and agree with everything I say."

"Garbage." Hope pulled her head back, forcing him to release her hair. The lock promptly curled back into the neat pageboy that fell just to chin level, its obedience a testament to the skill—and price—of her hairdresser. "I'm long past the age of thinking you're God, Nicky."

The childhood name weakened the impact of her words. She seemed to realize it and fixed him with stern green eyes to show she intended to be taken seriously.

"A pity," Nick said. "You were much easier to deal with when you thought I was God."

"The point is that you're walking right back into a situation where you're likely to get hurt," Hope said, ignoring his comment.

"I may not get hurt."

"Why take the risk?"

"Life's a risk, Hope. Didn't anyone ever tell you that?" His attempt at levity did nothing to lighten her expression. He sighed, his eyes suddenly serious. "Look, I don't know what Tess and I have, but it's something I've never experienced with anyone else."

"Typical man. Putting sex at the top of your priority list. It takes more than sex to build a relationship, Nick. You must have told me that a million times when I was a teenager."

"More like two million." He leaned his head back on the sofa and stared at the thick walnut paneling on the opposite wall without seeing it. "It's not just sex, Hope. There's something there—a connection of some kind. When I saw her at Fran McKenzie's party, it was..." His voice trailed off and he shook his head. "I don't know what the hell it was. But I want to find out."

There was a brief silence while Hope digested his words. "Did she tell you why she divorced you?"

"I didn't ask."

"Are you still in love with her?"

From the quick way she delivered the question, it was obvious Hope was trying to surprise some hidden truth out of him. But the question was hardly a new one to Nick. It was one he'd asked himself—more than once. He could only give her the same answer he'd come up with on his own.

"I don't know."

"You don't know?" Hope's tone was disbelieving. "How can you not know whether or not you're in love?"

"It's not all that hard." Nick's mouth twisted ruefully. It was obvious Hope had never been in love, he thought. "All I know is that I need to find out, once and for all, what the link is between us. And I don't want to hear a lot of flack from anyone in the family about it."

"So you called me in separately?" she questioned, raising her eyebrows.

"I know you're the one most likely to give me grief," he told her bluntly. "I'm not asking your permission, Hope. I'm just doing you the courtesy of letting you know what's going on."

She was silent a moment, digesting his words and the flat, matter-of-fact tone. "Well, I guess that puts me firmly in my place."

"You wouldn't know your place if it bit you on the nose."

"I hope this works out the way you want, Nicky," she said, her eyes suddenly turning serious. "I really do."

"Thanks, kid." Nick brushed his knuckles over her cheek, feeling a rush of affection.

"Well, even if I think you're doing something stupid—and I do—I want you to be happy."

"Thanks for the vote of confidence," Nick said dryly.

"You're welcome." Hope glanced at her watch and grimaced. "I've got a meeting with Ben Sinclair in half an hour and I need to go over my notes."

She stood up, smoothing her skirt into place. Nick eyed the length of leg exposed by the narrow black skirt with an older brother's disapproval but restrained the urge to comment. He had to admit, reluctantly, she had the legs for it.

"Don't let Sinclair buffalo you into lowering the bid. He tries it every time. To tell the truth, I think he'd be disappointed if he won."

"I can handle him." She said it with such confidence that Nick felt a swell of brotherly pride. Sometimes it was hard to remember that the cool, elegant professional he worked with was the same little girl who'd come to him with skinned knees and boyfriend troubles.

He walked to the door with her. Her hand on the knob, Hope hesitated.

"This thing with Tess is really important to you, isn't it, Nicky?"

"I don't know yet," Nick said, knowing that wasn't really true. It had been important enough for him to seek Tess out, even after three months. He wasn't sure he really wanted to look at just how important it might be. The look in Hope's eyes told him she recognized his hedging for exactly what it was.

"Don't rush her," she said abruptly. "If you want a chance to make things work, don't push too hard."

"Are you trying to tell me I'm normally pushy?" Nick asked, raising his brows.

"No. At least, not obnoxiously so." There was friendly spite in her smile but it soon faded. "I sometimes got the feeling from Tess that she felt a little overwhelmed by you. Maybe by the family, too. Tess wasn't inclined to open up much, at least not to me."

Nor to me, Nick thought, remembering old frustrations.

"But she said something once about all of us knowing where we were going," Hope continued. "That we all managed to be ourselves without disappearing in each other's shadows. I got the feeling that maybe she thought she disappeared in your shadow."

Hope's words lingered in Nick's mind after she'd gone. He sank into the chair behind his desk but he didn't reach for any of the paperwork that was waiting for him. Since his father's heart attack, he'd had plenty of opportunities to hone a natural talent for ignoring reports. Now, he put that talent to work, turning his chair to face the floor-to-ceiling windows behind his desk.

The Santa Ana winds had blown most of the night before, leaving the sky over Los Angeles a pale, clear blue. The temperature hovered in the mid-seventies. Hardly traditional Christmas weather, unless you were a native Angeleno.

Nick was only peripherally aware of the view spread out before him as he considered the idea that Tess might have felt overwhelmed by him. That had certainly never been his intention, not now and not five years ago.

Don't rush her, Hope had said. Well, maybe he had done that when they'd first met. But this time, he was determined to take things more slowly, to explore what, if anything, remained of the ties between them. No rushing into anything this time, he thought.

One day at a time and they'd see where it led them.

"TELL ME EVERYTHING." Josie punctuated the command by plopping her purse onto the floor next to her chair. Her pale blue eyes pinned Tess to her seat. "We were so busy when you got back yesterday and then I had to leave early. You didn't get a chance to tell me how your meeting with your ex-husband went."

"You mean you didn't get a chance to grill me," Tess corrected.

She dropped the catalog she'd been perusing onto the desk. She'd worry about ordering more crewel kits after the holidays when she had a better idea of what her inventory looked like. It had nothing to do with the fact that she hadn't been able to concentrate on anything since her meeting with Nick the day before.

"Grill has such a harsh sound," Josie said. "I prefer friendly interest."

"Let's face it, Josie, all you need is a rubber hose and a bright light for atmosphere." Tess reached for her cup of herbal tea.

"I resent the implication, Tess. You'd think I was nosy or something."

"You *are* nosy." Tess said it without malice. The truth was, Josie was the nosiest person she'd ever known. She wanted to know everything about everything and she rarely hesitated to ask personal questions. But her curiosity was backed by a genuine concern that made it impossible to take offense.

Josie tried to look indignant but the twinkle of laughter in her eyes ruined the attempt. "I'm not at all nosy. So what happened between you and Nick?"

The blatant contradiction drew a laugh out of Tess. "You're incorrigible, Josie, and I should fire you."

"You can't fire me. Union rules."

"What union?"

"The one I started. Now, talk to me. Did you tell him?"

"No." When Josie gave her a disapproving look, Tess raised her chin. "It's too soon."

"Not if you ask me." Josie got up and poured herself a cup of coffee from the pot Tess had made for her. Tess sniffed wistfully at the rich smell of it before sipping her own herbal brew.

"I didn't ask you," she said as Josie sat down again. "I'll tell Nick when the time seems right."

"So you're going to see him again?" Josie asked, catching the implication in Tess's words.

"Yes. We decided that, since there's obviously something between us—"

"More than he knows."

"—that we should see each other a little more," Tess continued, ignoring Josie's muttered comment.

"So you're going to start dating."

"Not dating," Tess denied. "Not really. We're just going to go out a few times. You know, get to know each other again, see how we feel."

"So when's the first date?"

Tess started to protest and then decided not to waste her breath. After all, on the surface, it did seem as if she and Nick were going to be dating. It would be impossible to explain to Josie how it differed. She couldn't even explain it to herself. She just knew she wasn't ready to put that term to what was happening between her and Nick.

Dating implied things. Things like beginnings and possibilities for the future. Scary things she didn't want to think about quite yet.

"Nick's picking me up tonight. He has tickets to see a performance of *A Christmas Carol* in Pasadena."

"Sounds like fun," Josie said. She glanced at the clock and stood up. "You look comfortable. Let me open up this morning." She lifted the keys off the hook where Tess kept them. "I think things are going to work out just fine for the two of you. I liked the look of your Nick."

Tess opened her mouth to say that he wasn't "her" Nick. Not anymore. But Josie was already out of the office. No doubt she'd planned her departure to leave no time to respond, Tess thought, mildly annoyed. If it wasn't for the fact that the older woman was her best friend, she'd be sorely tempted to fire her.

Her Nick.

He wasn't hers at all, she thought, reaching for an invoice. She wasn't sure he ever had been.

In fact, she'd always felt more like she belonged to him.

No, Josie had the wrong idea. She thought that Nick had come back into her life and that everything was going to work out the way it would in the movies. But life seldom imitated film. She knew that from personal experience.

They were just going to take things one day at a time and see where they went.

No promises. No expectations.

Just one day at a time.

THE SUNSHINE THAT had been bathing L.A. for the last three weeks of November had not made its usual appearance that morning. Instead, the sky had been overcast with clouds that threatened rain. The temperature had dropped and Southern Californians broke out their heavy coats to deal with the chilly, fifty-degree weather.

Nick was oblivious to the chill in the air. If it had suddenly snowed and delivered them a white Christmas season, he wouldn't have noticed.

He stood on the walkway in front of Tess's house—the house that had once been theirs—and had the odd sensation of time shifting around him.

Nothing seemed to have changed. The shutters and trim were still colonial blue, standing out against the barely yellow siding. They'd painted it themselves, though he could have afforded to hire professionals. But this had been their home, their first together, and they'd wanted to do the work themselves. It had taken days, but when they'd stood back to admire the results of their labors, it had been worth every aching muscle and paint-spattered shrub.

"Of course it's the same color," he muttered aloud now, hoping to release himself from his memory's spell. "Tess picked it. Why wouldn't she keep the same scheme?"

He continued up the walkway, resisting the elusive whisper of old memories, old dreams. The rosebushes Tess had planted that first spring were thick and bushy, some of them nearly as high as his head. A few late roses still clung to the canes, the pale colors standing out against the darkness like muted globes of light.

Stepping up onto the porch, he saw the old-fashioned swing in the corner and felt sweet remembrance pierce him. He'd hung the swing the first summer they were here. They'd spent a lot of lazy hours there, Tess's head on his shoulder, his arm holding her close as they rocked.

Odd, he didn't remember spending much time there after that first summer. He'd started traveling more for the firm that fall. When he was home, there always seemed to be so much to do, there just hadn't been much time for quiet pursuits like sitting on a porch swing. Maybe he should have made a point of making time.

A huge wreath of fresh evergreen boughs with a festive red bow hung on the door, giving off a crisp pine smell that he immediately associated with

Christmas. The Christmas they'd spent together, right here in this Victorian. The house had been decorated inside and out, gaily proclaiming the holiday that they anticipated sharing.

He shook his head, as if to dispel the memories. What was it Tess had said to him earlier? Oh, yeah. This wasn't the time for postmortems.

No past. No future. Only today.

It felt strange to be ringing the doorbell when he used to walk freely in and out of this same door. There was a short pause and then Tess was pulling open the door and Nick felt his pulse accelerate in a way that had nothing to do with the casually friendly attitude he'd determined to take.

"Nick." Just his name, certainly nothing to make him want to drag her into his arms and kiss her breathless. Nick forced down just that urge and smiled.

"TESS."

Tess's fingers curled over the door. How was it possible that just hearing her ex-husband say her name could make her pulse beat faster? Though if she were completely truthful, she wasn't sure her pulse had been completely normal since seeing him yesterday.

The porch light turned his hair to pale gold and cast his eyes in shadow, emphasizing the chiseled line of his jaw. He looked like nothing so much as a Viking warrior, come to claim a prize won in battle. For a moment, she wished that it were really that simple.

Wouldn't it be wonderful to be the helpless heroine in an old Errol Flynn movie, with Nick in the role of swashbuckling hero? He could sweep her up over his shoulder and carry her off and she wouldn't have to worry about whether it was a good idea. It wouldn't matter if she found herself disappearing in his shadow because the movie would end before it became important.

"Tess."

She blinked and found herself staring into Nick's puzzled eyes. A slow flush crawled up from her neck and suffused her cheeks. She must have been standing there staring at him as if she'd been struck dumb.

"Sorry. I didn't mean to space out on you."

Thank heavens he couldn't possibly know what had been going through her mind. He'd think she was nuts. And he'd probably be right.

"No problem. I feel like that after work sometimes. Rough day?"

She shrugged. "Christmas is busy for everyone."

"True. But it must be good for business."

"Yes."

There was a pause. Tess stared at Nick, racking her brain for something intelligent to say. But she seemed to have momentarily depleted her store of intelligent conversation.

"Can I come in?"

Nick's quizzical tone brought the color rushing into her cheeks again. She hadn't even realized they were still standing in the doorway.

"Of course. I'm sorry. I don't know where my brain is today."

Tess backed away so quickly, she stumbled over the throw rug that lay in the center of the entryway. Nick's hand shot out automatically, catching her elbow to steady her as he stepped inside.

"Thanks," she said, pulling away from his light hold. The breathlessness of her voice was only partially caused by her near fall. Her skin tingled where Nick's fingers had been.

"That rug always was a hazard," he commented. He pushed the door shut behind him, closing them in together.

"I suppose I should move it." Tess eased a little away, feeling as if the spacious entry had suddenly gotten much smaller.

"You've been saying that ever since we put it down," Nick said, grinning.

"Well, it looks nice there," she said defensively.

"You've been saying that, too."

"You just have no appreciation for aesthetics." She looked up at him, her eyes gleaming with laughter.

"And you have no understanding of practicalities."

"Plebeian."

"Romantic."

They grinned at each other, each swept up in the warm familiarity of the old argument, one they'd had often during their marriage. Then, as now, the point had never been for either of them to win or even to come to any solution. It had been a game they played, a way of confirming their closeness by perversely emphasizing their differences.

Of course, five years ago, the argument would have ended with a kiss. Tess's smile faded abruptly as she read the same awareness in Nick's eyes. She'd been uncertain about having him pick her up at home but it had seemed ridiculous to suggest meeting him somewhere else. But this was exactly what she'd been afraid of.

Here, in this house, where they'd built so many dreams—albeit on too fragile a foundation—it was all too easy to remember only the dreams and forget their ending. It was easy to forget there'd *been* an ending.

"It brings back a lot of memories, doesn't it?" Nick said softly. He'd read the haunting thoughts in her mind. "The two of us together in this house."

"Yes." Tess slipped her hands into the pockets of her pale gray slacks to conceal the fact that they weren't quite steady. "I almost suggested meeting you at the theater," she confessed, surprising herself.

"I almost suggested the same thing."

Nick's admission jerked her eyes back to his face. "You did?"

"I was nervous about picking you up here. I haven't seen the place since the divorce. I wasn't sure which would be worse—to find everything the way I remembered or to see everything changed."

"I guess I didn't change it all that much," Tess said, only just then realizing how little she *had* changed.

"I noticed."

"Does it bother you?" It was the first time she'd considered the idea that Nick might feel some of the same uncertainties she did.

He took his time answering, glancing around the entry hall, at the wallpaper they'd picked out together, at the gilded mirror they'd bought at the Rose Bowl swap meet and restored. Tess tried to see it through his eyes, wondering what it would be like to walk into a place that had once been your home and see the physical surroundings almost as they had been, even though the circumstances had changed completely.

"I like it," he said at last, his eyes coming back to hers.

Tess returned his smile and for some reason, the tension that had been between them since his arrival was suddenly eased. It was as if acknowledging the awkwardness they both felt had made it disappear. She wondered if the time would ever come when she was completely at ease with him again.

"It's going to take some time," Nick said, again reading her thoughts just the way she remembered.

"I know."

"It's worth it, Tess." He reached out to cup her cheek with one broad hand. "We can't walk away from this again."

"No." For reasons he couldn't even begin to guess, she thought.

"Maybe we can make it work this time," he said, his thumb brushing across her soft skin. It was perilously close to breaking their agreement that there would be no promises, no expectations, but Tess didn't protest.

She leaned her face into his hand, half closing her eyes. She wanted to believe they could make it work. More than he could possibly know.

Chapter Seven

Tess had had five years to forget how much fun her ex-husband could be. When she'd thought of Nick, she'd tended to focus on the negative: his traveling, the way she'd always felt overwhelmed by his drive, by his mere presence. At first, it had made it hurt less to think only of the bad things. After a while, it had become such a habit that she'd almost managed to convince herself that there hadn't been very many good things.

But it took less than two weeks to show her she'd been lying to herself. She'd forgotten Nick's ability to make her laugh, the way he never hesitated to laugh at himself.

She'd also concentrated so much on the way she'd often felt overwhelmed when he was around that she'd forgotten that she had also never felt safer or more cared for than when she was with him. It was a feeling to which she could easily grow accustomed.

What scared her was that it would be even easier to get accustomed to having the man himself around.

THEY HADN'T DISCUSSED the specifics of their tentative new relationship; things like how often they'd see each other had not been mentioned. Vaguely, Tess had thought that "taking it slow" might mean getting together once a week, maybe less considering the holidays.

Nick's idea of slow was altogether different.

On Thursday they went to see *A Christmas Carol*. On Saturday, they went to see a new animated Christmas movie in the company of what seemed like a thousand children. Watching Nick waiting in line at the snack bar, children eddying around him like windblown grass around an oak tree, Tess felt a pang. If they'd stayed married, would they have had kids of their own by now? What kind of a father would Nick be? Did he even want children? She realized she didn't even know.

They'd only discussed having a baby once during their marriage. Nick had said that he wanted to wait, to have some time for just the two of them before they expanded their family. Tess had agreed. After all, there was plenty of time to think about having a child. All the time in the world—or so she'd thought.

When their marriage hadn't worked out, she'd been doubly glad that they'd waited. The divorce had been hard enough without adding a child to the mix.

As Tess watched, a little girl tugged at the knee of Nick's jeans to get his attention. He bent down, listening with careful attention to whatever she was saying. When she opened her palm to display a handful of crumpled bills, it wasn't hard to guess that she wanted to know whether she had enough money to buy whatever candy she'd set her heart on.

The child's hair was almost the same color of golden blonde as Nick's. Anyone seeing them together would have assumed she was his daughter.

Seeing the picture the man and child made, Tess felt the sting of tears at the back of her eyes. Without conscious thought, her hand shifted, her palm flattening over her stomach.

Maybe...

No. She shook her head as if she could literally shake the disturbing questions from her mind. Not yet. It was too soon. Maybe after New Year's. If they were still seeing each other, maybe then.

"I WANT POPCORN and chocolate raisins and Milk Duds and a big Coke."

"That's an awful lot for such a little girl," Nick cautioned his small companion.

"Mama said I could order whatever I wanted while she was in the bathroom with Billy. He's my baby brother and she has to change his diapers all the time." A grimace accompanied this announcement, making her opinion of diapers—and maybe of baby brothers in general—perfectly clear. "Anythin' I want," she added, as if he might not have understood the first time.

Nick bit back a smile. Those serious eyes made it clear that a smile would not be appreciated at this point. He was no expert on children, but he guessed she couldn't have been much more than five. An adorable five, he added to himself. Big blue eyes, flaxen hair caught back from her face with a pair of lavender barrettes that just matched her dress, she could have persuaded the most confirmed child hater to soften his opinion.

He and Tess could have had a daughter this age, he thought suddenly. And she might have looked like this little girl, with his blond hair, her mother's eyes.

Odd that the thought should pop into his head now. They were a long way from thinking about children—if they were ever going to reach that point.

"Have I got enough?" the girl questioned him again, showing a touch of impatience with his apparent slow-wittedness.

Nick counted the crumpled bills in her hand. She had enough, but he couldn't help but wonder if her mother had intended for her to spend it all. Still, it wasn't his concern, and from the determined set of the child's chin, he doubted he could talk her out of her candy.

"You've got enough," he told her.

He was rewarded with a wide grin that revealed a matched pair of dimples and a set of pearly white teeth. He grinned back at her, feeling an odd little catch of emotion in his chest. God, what a feeling it would be to be responsible for a little charmer like this one, he thought. To watch her grow and learn. To catch a glimpse of the world through her eyes.

He straightened, his gaze seeking out Tess. Their eyes met and locked and Nick thought he saw something of his own thoughts reflected in her face. Did she ever think about the fact that they might have had a child about the same age as this girl? Did Tess wonder if their lives might have turned out differently if they hadn't decided to postpone having a family?

Did she care?

ON SUNDAY, Nick brought a picnic and they went to Griffith Park. Tuesday, he just happened to have tickets to see *The Nutcracker* performed at The Dorothy Chandler Pavilion. Wednesday, Tess insisted she had paperwork. It was the truth, though there was nothing she couldn't have put off another day or two. But she had the feeling she'd been caught up in a whirlwind, her life spinning out of her control. She had to take time to catch her breath.

But once she had the time, she found herself staring at the phone and thinking about calling Nick to tell him she'd changed her mind and wanted to have dinner with him after all. Pride kept her from picking up the receiver but pride couldn't prevent her thoughts from drifting in his direction. The paperwork sat on her desk, unnoticed and undone.

When Nick picked her up at the shop Thursday at closing time, it was to go on a tree-shopping expedition. Tess hadn't bothered putting up a Christmas tree since the divorce, thinking it would only serve to make her feel more alone.

"But it isn't Christmas without a tree," Nick announced, looking shocked.

Tess agreed. That suited her just fine. If it weren't for the brisk business that Christmas brought to her shop, she would be just as glad to avoid the holidays altogether. They held too many memories.

But somehow, Nick had convinced her that a tree was absolutely essential, and in no time Tess had found herself laughing and agreeing that the corner of the front room was indeed the perfect place for one.

An hour after Nick picked her up, he was struggling through the front door with an eight-foot Douglas fir that had no interest in compressing itself to fit through a doorway.

Tess wasn't sure how her "small" tree had grown so big, anymore than she could have said just why she'd agreed to having a tree in the first place. The only thing she was sure of was that she couldn't remember the last time she'd had so much fun.

THE SUNSHINE FOR WHICH Southern California was so justly famous had disappeared again at the beginning of the week. Temperatures dropped and heavy gray clouds blanketed the sky, promising rain but delivering little more than an occasional drizzle. Rain or no, the chill was enough to make a fire the perfect accompaniment to an evening spent trimming the Christmas tree.

Once Nick had muscled the tree into the stand, he piled wood into the grate and lit a fire. The flames were just starting to lick up over the logs when Tess brought in a tray of cocoa and cookies. She'd baked them the night before when she should have been doing the paperwork that was still piled on her desk.

Nick had been crouched in front of the fire but he stood up as she entered the room, turning toward her. He looked so right there, as if he belonged, as if the room needed his presence to be complete.

Like her life?

The thought slipped in so quietly that it was a moment before Tess felt its impact. The tray settled onto the coffee table with more force than she'd intended as her fingers seemed to weaken abruptly.

"You should have asked me to bring that in for you," Nick said, stepping forward and bending to slide the tray farther onto the table.

"It's not heavy," Tess said automatically. The scent of his after-shave didn't make it any easier to clear her unaccountably confused thinking. She straightened, hoping even that small distance would put everything into better perspective.

Her eyes fell on the way the gold of Nick's hair contrasted with the green of the sweater he was wearing, a green that matched his eyes to sinful perfection. The thin cashmere clung to the muscles of his back. Tess's fingers curled into her palms at the memory of the way those muscles felt under her hands.

"Cookies!" Nick's voice held unabashed greed. His eyes smiled in delight.

Tess blinked and dragged her thoughts to more acceptable paths.

"I thought they'd be nice with the cocoa," she said.

She watched as Nick's strong teeth bit into the soft sugar cookie shaped like a toy soldier. He chewed and swallowed, his expression as serious as that of an oenophile testing a fine cabernet.

"Fantastic," he pronounced.

"Thanks." Tess told herself the fact that it came from Nick didn't make the compliment any more important than it would have been from someone else. But the quick lecture didn't stem the warm tide of pleasure that washed over her.

Nick finished the first cookie with obvious relish and bent to take another one. "I haven't had cookies like this in years."

"If it's my baking you missed, I could give you the recipes," she said lightly.

"I missed more than your cooking."

"That's what they all say." She reached for her cocoa, only to have Nick's hand close over hers. Startled, Tess's eyes flew to his face.

"I didn't spend the last three months thinking about your apple pie, Tess." His tone was light, but there was nothing light about the look in his eyes.

"I believe you," she whispered, finding her voice nearly choked off by the sudden tightness in her throat. Believing that he was interested in more than her cooking skills wasn't the problem.

It was determining what he *was* interested in that had her tied in knots.

NICK WATCHED Tess's face, wishing he could read what she was thinking. But those beautiful blue eyes hid so much more than they revealed, just as they'd always done. He knew she didn't seriously believe he was only interested in her cooking, and he was becoming impatient with this game they were playing.

He didn't want to be Tess's friend. Or at least, that wasn't all he wanted. He wanted to be her lover. He wanted to feel he had some claim to her besides the extremely tenuous one of being her ex-husband. He didn't want to be her ex-anything. He wanted his presence in her life to be based on more than past connections.

Tess tugged on her hand and he released it. He watched as she picked up her cocoa mug, though he doubted she had any real interest in the steaming drink.

Patience, he reminded himself as her eyes flickered to his face and then away. It had been barely a week since he'd pushed his way back into her life. He couldn't expect to make up for five years in a few days.

"So, are we going to decorate this thing or leave it *au naturel?*"

He saw the tension ease from Tess as his light tone put them back on safe ground. It was like dealing with a half-wild kitten. She drew close only to dart away if he tried to tighten the fragile ties that bound them together.

Patience. A quality of which he'd never possessed any great quantity. But he was going to have to cultivate it if he wanted Tess back. And that *was* what he wanted.

Watching her open boxes of ornaments—ornaments they'd bought together, stored in the attic since the divorce—Nick determined that this was going to be only the first of many Christmases spent together. He still didn't know what had gone wrong before, why she'd wanted a divorce, but whatever it had been, this time they'd find a way to work it out.

He wasn't giving her up again.

"BE CAREFUL, NICK." Tess watched anxiously as Nick, perched on a stepladder, leaned over to slip the angel into her place on top of the tree.

"I'm not going to break my neck. Not after all this work." He leaned a little farther and set the angel in place.

"Actually, I was afraid you might fall into the tree and ruin it."

"Thanks for your underwhelming concern for my safety and well-being," he said dryly.

"Anytime."

Seeing the tuck in her cheek and the sparkle in her eyes, Nick wondered if it would be rushing things to drag her into his arms and kiss the smile from her mouth. Probably, he decided with an inward sigh. He folded up the stepladder and carried it to the back porch. When he returned, Tess was just clicking off the last lamp, leaving only the flickering firelight to light the room.

"Are you ready?" She hovered next to the outlet where the tree lights were to be plugged in.

"For someone who didn't want a tree at all, you sure are impatient."

Tess ignored his teasing remark and plugged the cord in. She stood up and backed away, coming to a stop beside Nick. They stared at the tree in silence. The colorful lights sparkled off the tinsel and were reflected in the ornaments. Nick had placed a single white lamp on the branch just below the angel and its pure light was reflected upward, giving her porcelain face a lifelike glow.

"It's beautiful." Tess's voice was hushed. She liked to think she was immune to the holidays, and yet, she couldn't pretend to be unaffected by the hope and promise that the glittering tree seemed to represent.

Or was it the hope and promise of Nick's presence that she felt?

"Not bad for two people who haven't decorated a tree in years," Nick commented.

"Not bad at all," Tess agreed softly. She could feel something dissolving inside, a hard knot that she hadn't even known was there until now.

It occurred to her that this past week had been one of the happiest she'd ever known. She'd divorced Nick because she'd been afraid she'd never be complete as long as she was in his shadow. Yet, with him gone from her life, there'd been a part of her missing.

"I think this calls for a toast." Nick picked up their cocoa mugs, which Tess had refilled just before they added the final touches to the tree.

"To Christmas," he said, his eyes holding hers.

"To Christmas," she whispered, knowing that neither one of them was thinking about Christmas.

She barely tasted the warm chocolaty drink. The room, which had always seemed quite spacious, was suddenly much smaller. The soft mutter of the fire wrapped them in intimacy, reminding her that they were alone.

They'd only spent one Christmas together in this house but the moment seemed filled with memories. Of all the Christmases they'd planned to spend together? Tess wasn't sure what it was, but she knew she hadn't felt this sense of rightness—of completion—in a long time.

Perhaps Nick read the feelings in her eyes, because he reached out to take her cocoa and set both cups on the coffee table. When he turned back to her, there was no mistaking the look in his eyes. Hunger. Need. And a question he didn't have to voice.

Nor did she have to give him her answer. At least, not in words.

NICK READ WHAT WAS in Tess's eyes and felt his heart start to pound in a heavy rhythm. He'd schooled himself to patience, promised himself he'd give her all the time she could possibly want. But her eyes were telling him that patience and time weren't what she wanted now.

His fingers found the red Christmas bow with which she'd tied back her hair, and tugged it loose. The ribbon drifted to the floor, a bright spot of color on the gray carpet. Loosened from its confinement, her hair fell in a heavy black curtain down her back.

"I used to dream about seeing you wearing nothing but your hair," Nick said quietly. He pulled a handful forward, letting it drape across the ivory linen of her blouse.

His hand came up to cup her cheek. His thumb brushed over her mouth and her lips parted in an invitation that echoed the look in her eyes.

"If I kiss you, Tess, I'm not going to want to stop," he whispered, his mouth only a heartbeat away.

"I'm not going to ask you to."

Nick's lips touched hers and the world was suddenly reduced to a space no bigger than the room that held them. Tess's mouth opened to him, her breath leaving her on a soft sigh as his tongue traced the soft line of her lower lip. Her hands came up to rest against his chest as she leaned into his strength.

As always, passion lay waiting between them, like kindling that needed only a match to set it ablaze. Nick flattened his hand against her spine, drawing her closer as his mouth hardened over hers.

Tess let herself melt against him, her fingers curling into his sweater, feeling the ripple of muscles beneath the fine cashmere. His tongue swept into her mouth, tasting her surrender. She gave him everything he asked and more, her body pliant in his arms, her tongue dueling with his in a battle neither wanted to win.

The hunger they had been trying to deny suddenly smoldered. It needed only a kiss to flare, and quickly the fire blazed out of control. Tess didn't care anymore. Just like it had been three months ago, there was only this man, this moment. And the knowledge deep inside her that this was right, that this was what had to happen.

No more regrets. No more pretending. Nick was the other half of her soul. She could no longer deny herself. Nor could she deny him.

In all her life, she'd only known true completion in this man's arms. For years she'd lived without it. Tonight, she was going to taste that completion again.

Heaven knew, the consequences could hardly have more impact on her life than those of that hot summer night.

NICK WAS NOT THINKING about consequences. He couldn't think beyond the soft miracle of having Tess in his arms again, of feeling her body bend to his, her hunger burning bright and hot to match his.

He'd wanted her so long. Like a starving man suddenly presented with a banquet, Nick was torn between conflicting urges. He wanted to drag every moment out, to savor each sigh, every touch. Yet he ached to sheathe himself in her and know the completion that he could find only with her.

Tess's hands slid up his shoulders, her slender fingers burying themselves in his thick gold hair at the nape of his neck as she rose on her toes, pressing herself closer, arching her body to his. Nick flattened his hand against her buttocks, letting her feel the aching ridge of his arousal. Her soft moan unraveled the fragile thread holding his control. With a groan, he crushed her to him, needing to feel her with every fiber of his being.

There was no question of right or wrong, no concern about future regrets. There was only the two of them, at this moment, in this place. Only the two of them and the hunger and need that had always drawn them together.

Clothes whispered to the floor. Neither of them could bear the time it would take to go upstairs to a bed. The thick carpet was bed enough. Nick's sweater provided a pillow for Tess. Her hair spilled over it, black against jade.

"You're so beautiful." Nick's voice was hushed as he looked at her. The firelight flickered over her skin, painting golden shadows on soft curves, teasing him by concealing even as it revealed.

"Don't make me wait, Nick." Tess's husky plea shivered over him, making him ache.

"Tess." Her name was almost a prayer.

His hips settled into the cradle of her thighs. Tess reached between them, her slim fingers closing over his arousal. Nick shuddered at the sweet torture of her touch as she guided him to her.

At the very threshold of paradise, he hesitated. Bracing himself on his arms, he looked down at her. Her face was flushed with passion, her eyes almost black with need. He could feel the moist welcome of her body, feel her hunger in the way her hands clutched at his hips, urging him to complete the union that lay only a heartbeat away.

Nick didn't doubt that her hunger burned as hot as his. But he wanted more than her passion. *That* had always been his. He wanted something more lasting, a promise toward the future.

"No regrets, Tess?" he asked, his voice husky. "No more running away?"

Her restless little movements stilled, her eyes locking on his. For a moment, the silence was so complete that the soft crackle of the fire seemed almost deafening.

Nick waited. Though it would damn near kill him to do it, he'd end this here and now unless she was as sure of the rightness of it as he was.

"No regrets, Nick." Her words were little more than a whisper but they were clear and steady. "And no more running away. Not anymore."

Nick felt relief wash over him. This wasn't the way he'd planned it. This was hardly a prime example of patience. But maybe patience wasn't what she needed, after all.

"Come to me, Nick," she whispered softly. "Make me whole again."

The invitation in her voice and the hunger in her eyes shredded the last ounce of his control.

"Tess." He sank against her with a slow thrust, feeling her heated dampness enfold him in the sweetest of embraces.

It was like coming home. It was completion. Wholeness. It was everything he'd remembered and so much more.

Tess shuddered under the impact of his entry. She'd asked him to make her whole again and he had. He'd filled her emptiness, made her complete. It was as if a part of her was his alone and she could only be complete in his arms.

In contrast to the urgency that had gone before, their lovemaking was slow and drugging. Nick set the pace—long, slow thrusts that drove the passion ever higher. The flames that crackled in the fireplace next to them were as nothing compared to the fire that burned between them.

He lowered his weight to his elbows, his broad chest gently crushing her breasts. Tess moaned as she felt his chest hair abrade her swollen nipples. Her hands slid up and down the length of his back, seeking something to cling to as the world spun madly around her.

It was too much, she thought feverishly. She would surely shatter in another moment. Yet she drew her knees up against his hips, taking him deeper still, needing to feel him in her very soul.

Nick wrapped his hands in her hair, holding her head still as his mouth devoured hers. His tongue thrust into her mouth, mimicking the rhythm of his deeper, more powerful thrusts. Tess whimpered against his mouth, her tongue twining hungrily with his.

The tension spiraled tighter and tighter, coiling low in her body until her entire being seemed focused on their joining. Her nails dug into his muscled back as she tore her mouth from his, her neck arching as the tension grew to unbearable proportions.

"Nick!"

His name was a plea. She was begging him to end the nearly painful sensations and yet praying they would never end.

Nick drew his head back, watching her face as he shifted the angle of his entry. He saw her eyes fly open, read the ecstasy there as the wave of completion caught her. And then she was melting against him.

His own climax was only a pulse beat after hers. The feel of her body tightening around him, caressing him in the most intimate of ways, sent him tumbling headlong into his own fulfillment.

Tess's pleasure was magnified a hundredfold by the feel of him shuddering inside her.

It was a long time before Nick gathered the energy to move from her. He hushed Tess's murmured protest with a kiss, his mouth lingering on hers. She didn't protest again when he slid an arm beneath her, tucking her head against his shoulder and drawing her to his side.

There were things to be said, but neither of them wanted to break the silence. Lying there, with the firelight flickering over their bodies and the soft glow of the Christmas tree in the corner, both were content to savor the moment. The questions could wait.

This was enough for now.

Chapter Eight

The Santa Anas began during the night, and by morning, the clouds that had hung over the L.A. basin for the past few days had dissipated, leaving clear blue skies and the promise of seventy-degree weather.

When Nick woke, sunshine was spilling through the light curtains, painting bright patterns on the polished oak floor and then tumbling over the pastel fabrics of the patchwork quilt that lay across the footboard.

The room hadn't changed a great deal since the days when he had shared it with Tess. The curtains were new but the wallpaper was the same ivory-and-blue floral stripe. The oak dresser still sat under the window but the bed in which they lay was no longer the huge oak frame he'd dragged up the stairs. Tess had never liked the bed and she'd replaced it with a brass frame that added a jaunty spark to the big bedroom.

It was the first time he'd awakened in this room in five years, yet it felt completely natural to be here. It was almost as if he'd been gone on a long business trip and had come home to find that Tess had rearranged the furniture. The differences were so minor that they hardly impinged on his consciousness.

Or maybe it was just that any bed would feel natural if Tess were in it, too.

Nick rolled onto his side and rose on one elbow, moving slowly to avoid disturbing her. She seemed to be deeply asleep, her breathing light and even. He couldn't resist the opportunity to look at her with all the barriers down between them.

Her lashes lay in dark crescents against her cheeks, a contrast to her sleep-flushed skin. Her mouth was soft and relaxed, her full lower lip tempting him to wake her with a kiss. Instead he feasted his eyes on the pure feminine beauty of her.

Her skin seemed to hold a gentle inner glow that he didn't remember from when they'd been married, as if she were lit from within. Her hair was scattered over the pillow beneath her, jet black against pristine white linen.

Nick traced his fingertip down one silken lock where it trailed over her shoulder, curving across the upper swell of her breast. From there, the temptation was irresistible. He nudged the sheet aside, exposing one dusky rose nipple. Tess stirred slightly, murmuring something unintelligible as he brushed his thumb over the soft bud, which puckered magically under the gentle touch.

He was tempted to lower his head and taste the response he'd elicited but he wasn't quite ready to have her awake. It had been a long time since she'd been his to look at and touch. He wanted to savor the moment.

At his urging the sheet slid down her slender body, baring her to the early-morning sunlight. He wasn't satisfied until the fabric had been banished to thigh level, leaving him an uninterrupted view.

God, but she was exquisite. From the tousled black satin of her hair his eyes trailed over each delicate feature. The winged darkness of her brows, the inviting fullness of her mouth, the fragile line of her collarbone. The fullness of her breasts had always seemed a delightful surprise on a woman of her slender proportions. They seemed even fuller than he remembered, a delicate tracery of blue veins just visible beneath her ivory skin.

Her waist was not as slender as he'd remembered either, and there was a gentle swell to her stomach that he'd never noticed. In his mind, he'd pictured her as being so slender that she hovered on the edge of being too thin. Nick half smiled, thinking that time distorted even the memories he'd thought most sharp.

By the time his gaze had reached the dark triangle of curling hair that marked the top of her thighs, a slow but intense arousal was building in him. Though they'd made love again after he carried her to bed the night before, his body obviously couldn't get enough of hers.

He cupped his palm around one soft breast, teasing the nipple to hardness with his thumb. Tess stirred but seemed reluctant to wake. Smiling, Nick bent to take her nipple into his mouth, nibbling gently until he heard her moan and felt the restless shifting of her legs. He lifted his head and looked down into her face, watching her lashes flicker once or twice before slowly lifting.

"Wake up, sleepyhead."

"Nick?" His name was a question, as if she couldn't quite believe he was really there.

"In the flesh." He grinned and dropped a quick, hard kiss on her mouth. "And I must say, Ms.

Armstrong, that you have very nice flesh indeed. I was just admiring it."

"Admiring what?" she asked, her eyes still sleepy.

"Your flesh. Every beautiful inch of it." He swept one hand from her shoulder to her thigh before letting it come to rest on the softness of her belly. "Daylight becomes you, Tess." She smiled, her lashes starting to drift downward as if sleep was still beckoning. Nick grinned, thinking that waking her up could prove to be a most rewarding activity. But he didn't get a chance to find out.

Tess's eyes suddenly flew open, her pupils dilated, something akin to panic in their depths. She sat up so suddenly that if Nick hadn't jerked out of the way, she would have banged her head into his. Oblivious to the near collision, she grabbed for the covers, snatching them up over her breasts and clutching them there as if her life depended on keeping them securely in place.

"Whoa!" Nick sat up beside her, rubbing one hand over his forehead as if half expecting to find a bruise. "What was that about?"

"Nothing."

"Nothing? You damned near concussed yourself on my head."

"I'm sorry." Tess's cheeks were deeply flushed, her eyes still showing traces of an inexplicable fear.

"I *have* seen you naked before," Nick said, eyeing her quizzically. "Just a few hours ago, if memory doesn't fail me."

"I know. I'm sorry." Her flush deepened, her eyes shifting away from his. "I guess it was just the idea that you'd been watching me while I slept."

"Sorry. It was irresistible." He grinned at her. "You look just as good as you did five years ago. Better, even. You've gained a little weight. It suits you. You always were on the thin side."

"Weight?" The color on her cheeks receded, leaving her suddenly pale.

"I think it looks great."

Nick wondered if he shouldn't have mentioned it. He wouldn't have if she hadn't thrown him so off balance. He was sincere in saying he thought the weight suited her, but you never could tell about women. They could be so touchy about their weight, turning five pounds into fifty in the mirror.

"I mean it," he said, when Tess didn't speak. "I think it looks good. You're even more beautiful than I remember."

Tess stared at him. "Thank you," she whispered.

There was a brief silence while Nick tried to think of something more to say. Tess sat there, clutching the sheet to her breasts, one hand pressed over her stomach as if to conceal the slight thickness there.

The way she was acting, you'd think he'd caught her in a lie, Nick thought. Or that she had something to hide. Some reason to fear what he might see, what he might learn.

Afterward, he'd never know where the thought had come from. There seemed no reason to think Tess's sudden skittishness was caused by anything more than the fact that, just as she'd said, it had startled her to think he'd been watching her while she slept.

No reason to think anything else.

But he was suddenly thinking about that almost luminous glow she seemed to have. About the slight thickening in her waist. About the new heaviness in her breasts and how sensitive they'd been last night when they were making love, his lightest touch sending shudders through her.

And about the fact that Tess—who'd always sworn she couldn't survive without caffeine to keep her going—was suddenly drinking decaffeinated coffee. And refusing even half a glass of wine, he remembered.

All the signs of pregnancy.

It was absurd. Maybe she was just cutting out caffeine for health reasons. And lots of people gained weight in the stomach. Half the men he worked with had guts and he'd never jumped to the conclusion that any of them were pregnant.

Yet the thought grabbed him by the throat and refused to let go. While logic told him he'd never had a stupider thought, every instinct was shouting that, logic or no, he was right. Tess was pregnant.

Feeling as if someone had slammed a fist into his gut, he dragged his eyes from that protective hand pressed to her stomach to her face.

And her eyes gave him the answer to the question he'd hardly managed to form in his mind.

She was carrying a baby. His baby.

TESS SAW THE KNOWLEDGE in Nick's eyes. He didn't have to say anything, any more than she'd had to tell him the truth. He knew. Without a word exchanged, he knew.

In a sudden flurry of panic, she started to swing her legs off the bed. She wasn't sure where she was going. Certainly there'd be no avoiding Nick, no pretending that he didn't know. There'd be questions she'd have to answer. But not right now, she thought. Later, when she'd magically come up with all the right answers. Then they could talk. But not now. Not right now.

As if she really had an option.

Nick's hand closed over her shoulder before she could get her feet untangled from the sheet. Tess tensed but she didn't try to resist the solid strength that pressed her inexorably back down onto the bed.

She did make a futile effort to retain her white-knuckled grip on the sheet when Nick started to pull it away, but he yanked it from her grasp, stripping it down, leaving her exposed to the emerald heat of his eyes. Totally vulnerable.

His palm flattened over her belly, testing the gentle swell, exploring it with a softness at odds with the emotions that hardened his jaw.

"It's true, isn't it?"

Her response was an instinctive, and foolish, attempt to put off the inevitable. "What's true?"

Nick's eyes swept to her face, burning with angry fire. "Don't lie to me, Tess. Not now. You're pregnant, aren't you? And it's my baby."

Tess opened her mouth to deny it, her only thought that she couldn't deal with this now. Not coming so quickly on the heels of last night's near paradise. She would have told him, she thought despairingly. Just not now. And certainly not this way. Just a few more days. Hours even. She just needed a little time to regain her equilibrium.

But it was clear that she'd run out of time.

"It's true." Her whispered confirmation seemed to echo, as if she'd shouted it.

"My God." The impact on Nick could not have been more powerful if her words had had actual, physical strength. He'd known, even before she said it. He wouldn't have believed the denial he knew she wanted to give him. Yet hearing her actually admit it left him without words.

He stared at her, the anger momentarily replaced by stunned disbelief. Illogically, he denied the truth he'd insisted she confess. "You can't be pregnant."

"Tell my doctor that," she snapped.

This time, he didn't try to stop her when she swung her legs off the bed. Tess glanced over her shoulder as she stood up but Nick didn't even seem aware of her departure. His eyes were focused on empty space, his features slack with shock.

Tess took advantage of his shock to grab her robe from the closet and pull it on. She felt a little less vulnerable with her body concealed from him, a little more capable of coping.

"When we were married, you were on the Pill," Nick said, still sounding as if he'd been hit with a baseball bat. He stared at her without really seeing her. "I didn't think... It seemed so much like old times...."

Tess closed her eyes, trying not to remember just how much like old times it had seemed. She didn't blame Nick for not thinking of birth control. She hadn't given it a moment's consideration herself. Like him, all she'd thought about was how right it felt, how much like coming home.

"I quit taking the Pill after the divorce," she told him.

Reluctantly, yet knowing she had no choice, she turned to face Nick. He still sat on the bed, one knee drawn up, the other leg bent beneath him. He seemed unconcerned with his own nudity. Tess wished it were as easy for her to ignore.

"How long have you known?" He sounded dazed, the reality of what she'd told him not quite sunk in. He didn't wait for her to answer but continued. "It's been three months. You must have known for weeks now."

Anger rose in his eyes, driving out the shocked disbelief. "You must have known for weeks," he said again.

Tess's teeth worried her lower lip, her eyes shifting away from his. She could hardly lie to him, tell him she'd just found out. Yet she couldn't bring herself to confirm the knowledge in his eyes—the realization that she'd known she was carrying his child and had chosen not to tell him.

"When were you going to tell me, Tess? When were you going to tell me about the baby?"

She tightened her belt unnecessarily and kept her eyes on the floor. What should she tell him? That she didn't know the answer to that question? That she didn't know the answer to any of the questions he had a perfect right to ask?

"When were you going to tell me you were pregnant, Tess?" His voice roughened. "Or had you decided not to tell me at all?"

Her eyes met his for a fleeting moment before she half turned from him, lifting one shoulder in an uncertain shrug. Another question to which she had no answer. She didn't *know* what she'd planned, hardly knew what she'd thought.

She heard Nick's bare feet hit the oak floor an instant before she felt his fingers close over her shoulder, turning her to face him. If it hadn't been Nick standing before her, Tess might have felt actual fear. The anger that blazed in his eyes and hardened his jaw to iron made him more than a little intimidating.

"*Were* you going to tell me, Tess?"

She met his eyes. She refused to cower, no matter how justifiable his anger.

"I was going to wait until after the holidays and see where we stood then." It had seemed so reasonable when she'd made the decision. Now, saying it out loud, it sounded weak and selfish.

"And what if things weren't going well between us? Were you just going to keep it from me?" Nick stopped, his fingers tightening on her arm as a new thought occurred to him. "You've known this for weeks already. What if I hadn't come to find you? Would you have called me to let me know I was about to become a father?"

"I don't know," she told him, giving him the honesty she should have given him in the beginning. "I don't know."

Nick's hand dropped from her arm as if she'd suddenly become too hot to touch. His eyes were filled with a sort of angry hurt that tore at Tess's heart.

"My God, what did I do to you that you'd keep something like this from me?" he asked hoarsely.

There was so much pain in the question that she reached out to him, wanting to take away the hurt she'd unthinkingly inflicted. He jerked away before her hand reached him as if her touch were acid, and gave her a look in which rage and pain were mixed in equal measure.

"It wasn't anything you did, Nick." Tess let her hand fall to her side, telling herself he had a right to his anger. "I just didn't know how to tell you."

"A phone call would have done nicely." Nick turned and grabbed his pants from the pile of clothes that they'd brought up with them the night before. Tess's blouse was tangled with them and he tossed it carelessly to the floor.

He stepped into the faded jeans and jerked them up over his hips, his mind spinning with what he'd learned.

Tess was pregnant.

That night three months ago they had created a child.

She'd known for weeks and hadn't told him.

He was going to be a father.

Each fact seemed separate and distinct, as if they had nothing to do with each other. He simply couldn't get his mind to grasp the reality of it. Neither the idea that she was having his baby, nor the fact that she'd chosen not to tell him about it. None of it seemed real.

"I thought about calling," Tess said.

Nick spun to face her, his face tight with fierce anger. "Is that what you were going to tell our child when he got old enough to ask why his father never came around? 'Gee, I meant to call and tell him. I just never got around to it.' "

Despite her determination not to cry, Tess felt her eyes sting with tears at Nick's savage tone.

"I don't know what I would have said."

"Maybe you figured you'd just let him think I don't give a damn about him. That would probably have been a lot easier for you. Fewer questions to answer."

"I wouldn't have done that," she cried. "I would never have let him think that."

"You'll forgive me if I don't take your word on that," Nick said, his icy tone as sharp as a knife.

"I wouldn't have let your son or daughter think you didn't care, Nick. You have to believe me."

"I don't believe you," he said coldly. "Lying to a man is not one of the best ways to gain his trust." Nick reached for his sweater and jerked it over his head.

"I didn't lie." Tess regretted the words the moment they were out. It was a weak defense and she knew it. The look Nick cut her told her he knew it, too.

"All right, so maybe I should have told you," she admitted.

"*Maybe,* Tess?" Nick's left brow disappeared into the heavy gold hair that lay on his forehead. "*Maybe* you should have told me?"

Nick saw the quick little gesture as she brushed away a tear and thought vaguely that he should be moved by her distress, that her regret should be enough to mollify his anger. Perhaps later, when he'd come to terms with the monumental changes in his life, then maybe he'd be more sympathetic.

At the moment, all he could think of was wanting to shake her until her teeth rattled. Along with that urge came another, just as strong. That was to hold her close and put his hand on her stomach, to feel the miracle of life growing inside her, the child they'd created together.

But she'd taken from him the right to do that, the right to share the miracle of it. All he could do was stand there and look at her through a veil of anger and hurt that was so thick, he wasn't sure it would ever dissipate.

"I'm sorry, Nick. I didn't mean to hurt you."

"For someone who wasn't trying, you did a bang-up job."

He wasn't giving an inch. Not now. Not yet. Maybe not ever.

"I was afraid," she whispered, her fingers twisting restlessly around the end of her belt, crushing the soft velour and then smoothing it out again.

"Of me?" he asked incredulously.

"Not exactly."

"Then of what?"

"I don't know," she admitted.

"There seems to be a hell of a lot you don't know," Nick snapped. "Is there anything you *do* know?"

"I know I didn't mean to hurt you."

He didn't need the tears that shimmered in her eyes to tell him that she meant it. He felt a tiny crack in the wall of anger he'd thrown up between them. But he was not yet ready to let the crack widen into forgiveness.

He wasn't sure he'd ever be ready.

"I have to go." The flat statement was the only response he could give her.

Tess's head came up, her eyes wide and startled. "Aren't we going to talk?"

"Coming from you, that's an interesting question." But the sarcasm was softened by a deep weariness. "We should have been talking weeks ago."

"I admitted I was wrong. I said I was sorry."

"Sometimes, sorry isn't enough, Tess." He looked away from her, glancing around the quiet room, his eyes lingering on the sleep-tousled bed. It didn't seem possible that less than thirty minutes ago, he'd awakened in that bed, feeling as if the world—his world—was getting back on track.

He thrust his fingers through his hair before sliding his hand to the back of his neck and squeezing the knotted muscles there. Tess stood there looking at him, her eyes wide and uncertain. He wanted to reassure her, to tell her they'd work everything out. But at the moment, he didn't know if that was going to happen.

"I'll be in touch," he said at last, knowing it wasn't enough. But it was all he could offer with any honesty. And God knew, honesty was one thing they needed right now.

"All right." Tess wanted to press him for something more definite. *When* would he be in touch? Where did they go from here? Did last night's intensity mean anything in the face of this morning's debacle?

She bit her tongue, holding back the questions. She'd have to wait and see what happened. Maybe that was to be her punishment.

Nick stared at her, obviously looking for something else to say. Perhaps he was as reluctant to end on such an unsatisfying note as she was.

"I'll be in touch," he said again, at a loss for anything more profound.

"I'll be here." She could hardly force her voice above a whisper but she was proud of its steadiness. At least, if she never saw him again, he wouldn't remember her as a sniveling child.

Tess thought he hesitated for a moment as he walked past her. For a wild moment, she thought he might take her in his arms and say that nothing mattered but that they'd created a baby together. But then he continued, the hesitation—if it had existed at all—gone.

She stayed where she was, listening as the bedroom door closed behind him. A minute later, she heard the front door close and then the sound of his car starting.

It wasn't until the engine's whine had faded completely that she moved. Feeling as if she were a hundred years old, she sank down on the edge of the bed. The faint musky scent of their lovemaking lingered on the sheets, rising up in a ghostly reminder of last night's passion. She closed her eyes against the acute pain that stabbed through her.

Against her closed eyelids, she could see Nick's face, hurt and angry. Her eyes snapped open, banishing the image. Staring at the wall opposite, she pressed one hand flat against the slight swell of her abdomen.

"What have I done?" she whispered.

But there was no answer.

Chapter Nine

The Christmas tree sparkled with light and color. Red and blue, green and gold, shiny silver from the strands of tinsel, the gleam of lights, and above it all, the serene porcelain face of the angel. It was a beauty that dazzled even as it soothed, excited even as it comforted.

"Tess."

Hearing her name, she turned, feeling a rush of joy and happiness when she saw Nick walk into the room.

"Nick."

"She wanted to see the lights," he said, looking down.

It was only then that Tess saw the infant he held cradled in his arms. She was wrapped in a gossamer-fine blanket of purest white. As Tess moved closer, seeming almost to float over the floor, the edge of the blanket fell back.

"Oh." The hushed exclamation was all she could manage. She had never seen a more exquisite baby in her life. Her beautifully shaped skull was covered by downy curls of a familiar gold and when she opened her eyes, Tess saw they were a pure clear green, seeming to hold a knowledge far beyond her tender age.

"She's beautiful," she whispered, reaching out to stroke one finger across the baby's cheek.

"Of course she is. She's ours. How could she be anything but beautiful?" Nick's voice was full of pride.

"She's ours?" Tess was filled with wonder. This *was the child she'd carried under her heart? The child she'd dreamed of holding in her arms?*

"Would you like to hold her?" As always, he seemed able to read her thoughts.

Tess nodded, holding out her arms to take the baby from him. The weight of her seemed to fill an emptiness she hadn't known existed until just that moment. The baby looked up at her with eyes just the color of her father's, eyes that were calm and steady.

"We did a good job on the tree."

At Nick's comment, Tess turned, looking up. The tree seemed, if possible, even more beautiful than it had a few minutes ago, as if having Nick and the baby there added something to its beauty.

"It's a wonderful tree," she said, feeling as if her world was absolutely perfect.

"I'm so glad the three of us are together." Nick put his arm around her shoulders, drawing her against his side in an embrace that encompassed both her and the baby. "It means so much to me, Tess, to be here like this."

"Where else would you be?" She tilted her head to look up at him, puzzled by his words. In the back of her mind, something stirred, a vague uneasiness that she couldn't quite put her finger on.

"Families should be together for the holidays," he said. "Fathers should be there."

"Yes."

She felt the weight of his arm easing from her shoulders as he stepped back. Or was she the one who'd moved?

"I want to know my child, Tess."

"Nick?" He seemed to be moving farther away.

"A child should have a father."

It was hard to distinguish his outline against the lights of the Christmas tree, which were suddenly glaring in her eyes.

"Nick?" She heard the fear in her voice. She wanted to reach out to him but she couldn't move her hands from the baby. She wanted to run after him but her feet seemed rooted to the floor. "Nick?"

"Don't tell her that I didn't care, Tess."

"I won't." She could no longer see him. She couldn't see anything but the harsh glitter of the tree, a mad swirl of colors and lights that loomed in her field of vision.

"Don't tell her I didn't care." The words were a whisper, rife with pain.

"Nick!"

There was no response. He was gone. And she knew he wouldn't be back.

Feeling as if there was only emptiness where her heart had been, Tess looked down at the baby she still held. The weight of her seemed less substantial, as if, with her father's disappearance, she'd lost something. The green eyes that looked up at Tess held a question.

"I didn't mean to hurt him," Tess whispered. "I didn't mean it."

But the question in those eyes had become an accusation and Tess knew she'd never be able to explain, never be able to make her understand.

Just like Nick would never understand....

TESS WOKE WITH A START. She sat bolt upright, her eyes flashed open and her heart pounded furiously. It was several seconds before her eyes took in her surroundings, the familiar surroundings of her bedroom. She was lying in her own bed, illuminated only by a soft pool of light from the bedside lamp.

It was just a dream, she told herself. *Just a dream....*

Her hand settled on the bulge of her belly and she squeezed her eyes shut, trying to force back the tears that burned at the backs of her eyes.

But all she saw emblazoned there was the burning image of Nick and the stark hurt on his face when he accused her of hiding her pregnancy. The absolute wonder in his eyes when he touched her stomach. The total disappointment when he walked out the door three days ago.

Unable to sleep, she got up and walked into the living room, as if drawn there. Moonlight streamed in through the open drapes and was caught and refracted over and over again by the strands of tinsel, making the tree shimmer with a life of its own. She felt oddly compelled to plug in the lights, and soon the tree was aglow with the colorful bulbs.

She and Nick had had so much fun decorating the tree. Laughter and the inevitable arguments about where to hang the lights had reminded her of the good times they'd once had. And hinted at what they could have again.

But in her dream Nick didn't hang around long enough. Like a spectre, he was suddenly gone, leaving her calling out to him, leaving the baby looking up at her with accusing eyes.

But it was just a dream, she told herself again.

She couldn't answer when the niggling voice inside her head asked, *Wasn't it?*

BY THE AFTERNOON, Tess was no closer to answering that question. She'd forced herself to eat something, knowing the growing baby needed nourishment, and she'd just finished mixing the ingredients for a batch of Christmas cookies. During December she made it a point to keep the shop stocked with fresh coffee and cookies. Usually she bought them, but today baking seemed a good antidote to the blues that threatened her. But her heart simply wasn't in it.

When the doorbell rang, she was almost grateful for the interruption. She set down the mixing spoon and wiped her hands on a towel as she went to the door. It was probably the elderly woman next door dropping in for a chat, as she often did. Tess pulled the door open without confirming her guess. When she saw who was on the other side, her welcoming smile vanished and her eyes widened with sudden uncertainty.

"Nick."

"HELLO, TESS." The flat greeting was all Nick could force out.

On the way over, he had wondered what he would feel when he saw her again. A deep anger still boiled in his gut, an anger like he'd never felt before.

But seeing her now, his first thought was not of how angry he was with her. It was of how beautiful she was. And how in awe he was of the miracle they'd created together. He wanted to press his hand to her stomach, to feel his child growing within her. But they were a long way from that moment, if they were ever to reach it at all.

The mixture of feelings made his voice flat, his tone cooler than he'd intended.

"How are you?"

"I'm fine." She brushed a tendril of hair back from her forehead, looking uncertain. "Would you like to come in?"

"Thank you." Nick stepped past her and into the entryway. He felt the same welcome from the house that he'd felt the day they'd first seen it. It seemed that no matter what passed between them, this house still felt like home. He pushed that thought aside and turned to face Tess.

"Would you like a cup of coffee?" she asked.

"Is that good for the baby?" The question came out sharper than he'd intended, sounding accusatory.

Tess raised her chin, her dark blue eyes showing a touch of annoyance. "I haven't had coffee since I found out I was pregnant. But the fumes are hardly likely to be a problem if I make some for you."

"Sorry. I didn't mean to sound pushy. I guess this whole idea has thrown me off balance."

"Babies have a tendency to do that," Tess told him, trying to regain a polite tone. "You get used to it after a while."

"Do you? I haven't had time to find that out."

The cool reminder extinguished her tentative smile like water thrown on a lit match.

"I suppose you haven't," she said expressionlessly.

There was a tense silence and then Nick exhaled abruptly. "I'm sorry, Tess. I shouldn't have said that."

"It was the truth."

"Maybe, but we're not going to get anywhere by beating a dead horse."

"Are we going to get anywhere if we don't beat it?" she asked carefully.

The second the words were spoken she regretted them. Why had she asked him that? It wasn't the time for talk of the future. She remembered the tiny life growing inside her belly and thought maybe it was too late.

Nick looked at her, his eyes brooding. All he said was "I don't know."

Tess started to say something but he shook his head, stopping her. "I don't want to talk about it right now. I just came over because I said I'd put up the lights."

"Lights?" Tess stared at him blankly, unable to follow him. "What lights?"

"The outdoor Christmas lights. I said I'd put them up for you."

"You came over to put up the Christmas lights?"

"I said I would," he repeated doggedly.

"I haven't had lights in years, Nick." It was not so much a protest as an expression of bewilderment. After the way they parted three days ago, the last thing she'd expected was to have Nick show up to hang Christmas lights. "You really don't need to go to all that trouble."

"It's no trouble."

Looking at the determined set of his jaw, Tess decided to give up the argument. For whatever reason, Nick had made up his mind that the house was going to be decorated for Christmas. If this was what he'd chosen as the first step toward them working out their problems, then it was easy enough to accommodate him.

"The lights are in the attic."

"Is the ladder still in the garage?" Some of the tension seemed to go out of him, as if he was relieved at her acquiescence.

"On the rafters." *Where you left it five years ago.* But she didn't say that out loud. The balance stretching between them was too fragile.

THOUGH TESS WOULDN'T have believed it possible, the afternoon passed pleasantly enough. She returned to her cookie baking while Nick clambered over the outside of the house, putting up lights. He even climbed up on the roof and set up the plastic Santa and all his reindeer that had graced the house the one Christmas they'd spent here together.

"Where'd you dig those things up?" Tess called to him on the roof when she went out to check his progress. "I'd even forgotten we had them."

Nick swung around toward her voice, almost losing his footing.

"I'm sorry," she said, knowing she'd startled him. "I didn't mean to intrude. I just came out to see if you wanted anything."

Even from up on the roof, his eyes bore into hers. "No, I'm fine" was all he said, and he turned back to the Santa.

On the way back into the kitchen, Tess could still feel those eyes on her.

She turned on the radio, which was playing the inevitable Christmas melodies, and started rolling out another batch of sugar-cookie dough on the counter. The occasional thump of the ladder against the side of the house reminded her of Nick's presence, and she was aware of a fragile feeling of contentment.

As she cut out reindeers and angels and chubby Santas, Tess thought about the baby she carried and how wonderful it would be if her child—their child—were to grow up in a home with two parents who loved each other. Just like her dream last night.

Not that she was ready to say she loved Nick, she told herself hastily. It hadn't even been two weeks since he'd come back into her life. It was premature to start thinking about love.

You fell in love with him quicker than that the first time, a sly voice whispered in her mind.

"And look where that ended," she said aloud.

Did *it end? Did you* ever *stop loving him?*

But that was a question she wasn't prepared to answer for anyone, not even herself.

BY THE TIME the sun started to sink toward the Pacific, Tess had baked half a dozen batches of cookies, enough to keep even the most voracious hordes of Christmas shoppers at bay for a day or two. She was just sliding the last sheet of cookies out of the oven, when the overhead light went out with a pop.

"Damn." She set the tray on top of the stove and shut the oven door. The only light in the room came from the fluorescents beneath the upper cupboards, and what little the setting sun cast through the west window.

Knowing it was silly, Tess wiggled the switch up and down a few times. The light remained off and her kitchen remained in gloom. Muttering under her breath, she got a light bulb out of the cupboard and dragged a chair under the fixture.

She had just reached up to unscrew the old bulb when she heard the back door open. Twisting her head to look behind her, she saw Nick step into the kitchen. Saw, also, the look of horror on his face.

"What the hell are you doing?" His tone could only be described as a bellow. He didn't bother to give Tess time to respond. He crossed the kitchen in three long strides and swept her off the chair.

Tess cried out, startled, and threw her arms around his neck. The bulb she held in her hand smacked into Nick's ear.

There was a moment of silence where Tess could hear the accelerated beat of her pulse. Or was it that she could feel Nick's heartbeat where she lay against his chest?

"What were you trying to do?" The bellow had become a growl but his displeasure was obvious.

"I was trying to change a light bulb," she said deadpan.

Tess pushed against him in a silent demand to be released. He seemed to hesitate for a moment, as if not sure she was safe to be allowed on her own. She drew her head back, glaring at him in the dim light, annoyed with him because he'd frightened her. Annoyed with herself because she didn't really want to leave his arms.

Reluctantly, Nick lowered the arm beneath her knees, bending to set her on the floor. Even then, he kept his arm behind her back, as if prepared to sweep her up again should she show any signs of toppling over.

"I realize that. What I meant was, what were you doing on that chair?"

"I was changing a light bulb," Tess said again, tugging her shirt back into place, smoothing it over her jeans.

"You were standing on a chair." He made it sound as if she'd been doing acrobatics.

"That's how I reach the old light bulb so that I can replace it with the new one." She held up the new bulb for emphasis.

"You shouldn't be standing on a chair."

"Well, it's easier than leaping up there and clinging to the fixture by my teeth while I change the bulb," she said with an insultingly sweet smile.

"You could have fallen." His scowl told her that her sarcasm was not appreciated.

"I've been changing light bulbs my whole life and I haven't fallen yet."

"You haven't been pregnant your whole life, either," he snapped.

There. He'd said it. The subject they'd tiptoed around all afternoon.

Dead silence hung between them as they faced each other in the darkened room. Their eyes were locked, as if each was trying to gauge the other's reaction.

"I'd make the record books if I had been," Tess said finally. "I don't think even elephants are pregnant that long."

Nick's smile came reluctantly but it *was* a smile. "That wasn't exactly what I meant."

"That's what it sounded like."

"I guess it did."

The momentary humor faded but it had served to break the finely drawn tension that had been between them all afternoon. There was a pause and then Nick's hand came out to flatten against her stomach in an almost convulsive gesture. Tess caught her breath at the touch but she didn't move away.

"God, Tess, I can't believe we're going to have a baby."

The breath she'd been holding all day came out on a sigh. "I thought maybe you'd forgotten," she said. She felt shaken to the core by his touch and the look of wonder in his face.

"It's all I've thought about." He didn't lift his eyes from her stomach, his fingers moving caressingly, as if touching the infant she carried. "Have you felt him move yet?"

"It's a little early for that. And it could be a her, you know."

"Either way. As long as she's healthy." Nick raised his eyes to hers. "What does it feel like, to know that you're carrying another life?" His hunger to share this with her was obvious.

Tess felt a pang of guilt. She'd been so wrong.

"It feels like a miracle," she said softly. Her eyes stung with tears as she set her hand over his. "I'm sorry, Nick. I should have told you about the baby. I'm so sorry."

"Why didn't you?"

There was no anger in the question, only a genuine need to understand. Here in the dimly lit kitchen, filled with the homey scent of baking, there didn't seem to be any place for anger. The time for anger was past. What each sought was to understand the other.

"I'm not sure," Tess said slowly. She tried to remember why it had all seemed so clear at the time. "At first, I was hurt that you hadn't called or come to see me. I know that was stupid." She gave him a shaky smile. "I was the one who ran away. I should have been the one to call. I guess I'm not as liberated as I like to think."

"No one said emotions are logical." Nick shrugged.

The movement seemed to remind him he was still touching her. His hand fell from her stomach and he stepped back.

Tess felt a deep sense of loss, as if he'd taken away a part of her. At the same time, she was grateful for the extra bit of distance between them.

Her thought processes had never been at their best when Nick was too close.

"I can understand that maybe, when you thought I was ignoring what had happened between us," he said slowly, obviously not at all sure he believed what he was saying but trying to be generous. "But what about later, when you knew about my father? When you knew what kept me away? Why didn't you tell me then, Tess?"

She hesitated, knowing she could never make him understand how much it had frightened her to think of letting him back into her life. It was something she only partially understood herself. So she offered him a partial truth.

"I guess I wasn't sure you'd be interested."

"Not interested!" Nick stared at her in disbelief. "What kind of man wouldn't be interested in his own child?"

"My father." She hadn't intended to say the words out loud but there they were, hanging in the air between them. Nick's eyes widened in surprise and then a look of understanding came into them. She looked away, annoyed with herself for revealing something she'd tried very hard to forget.

"I'm not your father, Tess," Nick said quietly. "I could never ignore my child. Don't you know me better than that?"

"Yes, I do. I guess I just wasn't thinking very clearly. One day we were divorced and out of each other's lives and the next I was carrying your baby—and somehow we skipped all the steps in between."

"All those steps in between aren't always necessary, Tess. Sometimes, you know what's right without them."

Maybe he knew, but all she was sure of was that, when it came to Nick Masters, she'd made a habit of going from point A to point Z without making any stops. And each time she arrived at the end she was out of breath and wondering if she'd made a mistake.

"I'm sorry I hurt you, Nick. That was never my intention."

"What's done is done." Nick shrugged and gave her a half smile. "I'll recover. What's important now is, where do we go from here?"

It was meant as a rhetorical question. He was thinking out loud. But Tess chose to answer it.

"I don't now. Where do you think we should go?"

Well, that was putting the ball squarely back in his court, Nick thought. The problem was that he wasn't quite sure what to do with it. Where *did* he think they should go from here?

"I want to be part of my child's life," he said slowly.

"But not of mine?" Tess lifted her chin, as if bracing for a blow.

"That's not what I meant." Nick thrust his fingers through his hair, trying to articulate feelings he hadn't yet clarified in his own mind. "My feelings for you haven't changed. I don't like what you did but I don't hate you for it, either. I...care about you."

The phrase was hopelessly inadequate. An anemic word like "care" didn't even begin to describe what he felt about her. But it was the best he could come up with at the moment.

"I care about you, too," Tess said, her voice hardly more than a whisper.

They looked at each other, each grateful for the poor light that concealed their own expressions while regretting that it hid the other's.

The air was pregnant with things unsaid, only half-understood. Nick wanted to pull her into his arms and hold her close. But it was too soon for that, for both of them. They needed time.

It was Nick who looked away first, glancing up at the dark light fixture.

"Why don't I change that bulb for you?" The prosaic offer was just what was needed to ease the tension before it became uncomfortable.

He stepped up on the chair and unscrewed the old bulb, handing it down to Tess and taking the new one from her.

"Thank you," she said as he jumped to the floor. "But I really would have been just fine."

"Maybe. But I'd rather you didn't go climbing on chairs, at least not as long as I'm around to do the climbing for you."

But you won't always be around. Tess didn't say the words out loud. She didn't have to. The same thought was in Nick's eyes.

For a moment, she thought he was going to say something and she held her breath, hoping for— What? She didn't even know what she wanted him to say.

But he turned away without speaking, leaving her with an indefinable feeling of something lost.

But you can't lose something you don't really have, she told herself.

Nick flipped the wall switch, and the kitchen was bathed in light. Painfully bright light. Tess blinked and looked around the room as if seeing it for the first time. The racks of cookies cooling on the counter, the canisters and mixing bowls beside them, all seemed to be part of someone else's life. It seemed like hours since she'd taken the last cookie sheet out of the oven, though a glance at the clock showed her it had been only a few minutes.

"That's better," Nick said, letting his hand drop from the switch.

"Is it?" Tess wasn't referring to the light.

"Yes." The strength of Nick's answer told her he knew what she was talking about. "We'll just go back to where we were."

"I don't think that's possible." She shook her head slowly. "I don't see how we can go back and pretend." Her doubt was painfully obvious.

"We don't have to pretend. We'll just do what we planned to do in the first place. We'll take things one day at a time and see where it goes from there."

"All right." It was, after all, the only choice. The baby linked them even without whatever it was that kept drawing them together.

"There's more drawing us together than the baby, Tess." Her flush revealed just how accurately he'd read her mind.

There might be more than a baby drawing them together, but there'd always seemed to be just as much pushing them apart. Tess brushed a tendril of hair back from her forehead, suddenly achingly tired.

Looking at her porcelain pale skin and seeing the subtle slump of her shoulders, Nick wanted to cross the room and take her in his arms and tell her everything was going to be all right.

"I'd better get going." He glanced at his watch as if just remembering somewhere he had to be. The truth was, the only appointment he had was with a TV dinner and a book.

"Of course." Tess straightened her shoulders with a visible effort. "Thanks for putting up the lights."

"You're welcome." They both knew the lights had merely provided him with the excuse he'd needed to come over.

There was an awkward little silence. They looked at each other across a few feet of polished oak floor that might as well have been the Grand Canyon. The distance was proving as uncrossable.

After a moment, Nick moved toward the door. Tess followed him into the front entry, not sure which she wanted more: to throw her arms around him and beg him not to go, or to see the door close behind him so that she could crawl up to bed and collapse.

Luckily for her muddled state of mind, she didn't have to make the choice. Nick paused before opening the door and turned to look at her.

"I'll call you."

"Okay."

He reached behind him for the doorknob but didn't immediately open it. "You'll be all right alone?"

"I'll be fine." She could have pointed out that she'd been alone for years, but there seemed no point to it.

"Try not to worry. We'll work it all out."

"Yes." It was easier to agree than to argue.

"I'll see you soon."

As if he couldn't stop himself, he reached out, brushing his fingers over her cheek in a caress so fleeting, she almost thought she'd dreamed it. Before she could respond, he'd pulled open the door and left, leaving her staring at the blank panel.

It wasn't until she'd heard his car pull away from the curb that she gathered the energy to move.

She was sure there were all sorts of things she should think about. Things to do with her and

Nick, things to do with her and Nick and the baby. But at the moment, all she wanted was a warm shower, a soft nightgown and a firm mattress.

Like Scarlett, she'd think about everything else tomorrow.

Chapter Ten

"Can you give me a hand?"

The question came from behind him. Nick turned, not sure it had been addressed to him. A middle-aged man smiled at him from the bed of a battered pickup. Seeing that the request *had* been directed at him, Nick walked toward the truck.

At this point, any distraction was welcome. He'd been standing across the street from Tess's shop for five minutes, debating the wisdom of going in. The two days since he'd seen her last seemed like two weeks. He found himself wondering if her pregnancy had become any more obvious, even though it seemed unlikely that two days would make an enormous difference.

"If you could just take that end of it, I'll get this one."

Nick looked into the bed of the pickup at a stack of plywood that had been painted red, with thin black lines drawn on it to indicate bricks.

"What is it?" he asked, as he slid his hand under the sheets of wood.

"Santa's house." The old man lifted the other end of the stack and walked the length of the bed with it. He set it on the tailgate and jumped into the street before picking it up again.

"Santa's moving to a warmer climate?" Nick questioned, following the other man's lead as they rounded the corner of the stationery store.

"Just making a visit. Here. Lean it against that lamp pole."

Nick followed his instructions and set the house-to-be down. Stepping back, he dusted his hands together and turned a critical eye on his companion.

"Don't tell me you're one of the elves? You don't look a thing like I expected."

"Not an elf." Blue eyes laughed at him from under dark brows liberally sprinkled with gray. "I'm Santa himself."

"You're Santa?" Nick eyes went automatically to the man's nearly nonexistent hairline before giving his clean-shaven features and slight build a doubtful look. "You're not what I expected, either."

"The wonders of makeup," he was told with a laugh. "Thanks for the help."

"You're welcome."

For lack of anything better to do and because it gave him a legitimate excuse to delay making a decision about seeing Tess, Nick followed him back to the pickup. If the man was surprised, he didn't reveal it. He merely gestured to a big wooden chair and lifted a box himself.

"You play Santa for the kids?" Nick asked as they carried the chair and the box to where they'd set the plywood.

"Sure do. I've been the Santa on this corner for eight years now."

He began assembling the little wooden shack that would be Santa's house for the next couple of weeks. It was obvious he'd done this so many times that he didn't need assistance. Still, Nick lingered.

"You like working with the kids?"

"Most of the time. Like anything, there's an occasional bad day where all the little ones do is cry and all the older ones want to do is pull your beard off to see if you're really Santa Claus."

Nick laughed with him but his eyes drifted across the street to the colorfully decorated front windows of Needles & Pins. Would Tess be glad to see him?

"Any kids of your own?" The friendly question drew Nick's attention back to Santa.

"We're expecting our first," he said slowly.

"Now that's a scary time. Exciting but scary, too." He unfolded the sides of the building, which were attached to the back with hinges. Nick helped him balance the little shack while he eased the supports into place.

"You have children?" Nick asked.

"Two. And one grandchild, born last spring. She's cute as the dickens but I don't envy my son and his wife a bit. It's a tougher world out there than it was when my two were little. Everybody expects so much of everybody else. And of themselves."

"Yeah." Nick's attention had drifted across the street again and he missed the shrewd look his companion gave him as he positioned Santa's chair in front of the plywood house.

"I wouldn't worry too much. I guess people have raised kids in tougher times. Not that it does much good to know that. You still worry yourself to death. Especially with the first one. You're not quite as bad with those that come after."

At the moment, Nick's only concern was the first one. And his or her mother. And where he was going to stand with both of them. He sure wasn't going to get any closer to finding out by lurking across the street from Tess's shop.

He said his farewells to his new acquaintance and started across the street, uncertain whether he felt like Sherman marching to conquer Atlanta or Napoleon about to meet Wellington.

TESS LOOKED UP as the bell over the door jangled and felt the familiar catch in her heartbeat when she saw Nick enter the shop. It took a considerable effort to return her attention to the customer in front of her.

"I wish I could help you, but it's just not possible to get a pillow finished for you in time for Christmas." She turned and gestured to the cross-stitched sign that announced the schedule for sending items out for professional finishing. "The end of October was the last possible date."

"But I just got the top done," the woman protested, as if that should be the only consideration. She tapped her fingers on the needlepoint canvas spread out on the counter.

"I'm sorry." Tess's smile was regretful but firm. "It's an original. I painted the canvas myself."

"It's lovely," Tess said, hoping her nose wouldn't grow from telling such a lie. She glanced at Nick, who'd stood close enough to listen to the conversation, and saw his brows go up as he looked at the needlepoint picture of a naked woman holding a bunch of grapes. The colors were garish and the stitching was sloppy. But Tess wasn't in business to tell her customers to find another hobby.

"Perhaps you could have this finished as a Valentine's gift?"

The suggestion made the woman's frown ease. A few more minutes of discussion and lamentation over the unreasonableness of people who couldn't drop what they were doing to finish an obvious masterpiece and she'd agreed that maybe Valentine's would be better after all.

Tess filled out the paperwork and carefully rolled the canvas under the woman's eagle eye. Another promise that it would be ready by the first week in February and the customer departed.

"Who's she giving it to? A madam?"

Nick's dry question made Tess grin. "Her son and daughter-in-law."

"You're kidding."

"No. She says it will be perfect for their decor."

"Early American bordello?"

"Could be," she said with a laugh. She finished putting a tag on the canvas and set it on a shelf behind the counter before turning back to Nick. What would she say to him?

"I know I said I'd call you," Nick said, breaking the silence before it could stretch too far. "But I happened to be in the area and thought I'd drop by instead. I hope you don't mind."

"Not at all. Are you on your way to a construction site?"

"How'd you know?"

"I assume you don't dress like that to go to the office," she said, gesturing to his black jeans and work boots. He wore a green-and-black buffalo plaid shirt with them. His golden hair was tousled just enough to make her fingers curl with the urge to tidy it. He looked, as he always did, devastatingly handsome.

Tess smoothed a hand over her hair, wishing she'd done something more elaborate with it and her clothes, too.

"I'm on my way to a project up near Angeles Crest," Nick was saying. "The client wanted a mansion built into the side of a mountain. Worst building site I've seen in years. Makes me glad I only have to design the things, not try to build them."

"But I bet you managed to design something spectacular *and* buildable," she said, knowing it was no more than the truth.

"I don't know about spectacular, but I came up with a modest little seven-thousand-square-foot cottage that seemed acceptable."

"*Only* seven thousand square feet?" Tess raised one dark brow in disdain. "Paltry."

Nick shared her smile, wondering if she had any idea how lovely she looked. She was wearing another of those loose jumpers, this one in a soft yellow that made him think of daffodils and springtime. Her hair lay over her shoulder in a thick black braid. His fingers tingled with the urge to loosen it from its confines and see it tumble over his hands.

But now was not the time for that. They were supposed to be taking things slow, finding out where they could go from here. And while going straight to bed held a definite appeal, it was hardly the answer.

"Actually, I'm glad you dropped by," Tess said. "I was thinking about calling you."

"That would be a change." But there was no anger in Nick's dry comment.

"I have a doctor's appointment tomorrow afternoon and I thought you might want to come along."

"Is something wrong?" Nick's hands gripped the counter as he leaned toward her, his features suddenly taut with worry.

"No. It's just a checkup. I know Dr. Kildare wouldn't mind if you came along."

"Dr. who?" Nick's tone made it clear that he thought he was hearing things.

"Dr. Kildare," Tess repeated, lifting her chin. "She happens to be an excellent ob/gyn. There *are* people named Kildare, you know."

"But not doctors," Nick said, laughing. "Why doesn't she change her name to Hossenfeffer or Geizendorfer? Something nice and normal."

Tess laughed reluctantly. "I admit I had my doubts but she's really very good."

"I'll take your word for it. I don't have much experience with ob/gyns."

"I guess not."

"What time is the appointment?"

"Five o'clock. Don't feel like you have to come just because I asked," she added quickly. "I just didn't want to shut you out."

Like I did before lay unspoken between them.

"I'd like to be there. If it won't bother you."

"No. That's fine. Just fine." Tess let her voice trail off, thinking that they sounded more like strangers than like two people who'd once been married, two people who were expecting a child together.

NICK WAS THINKING much the same thing as he left the shop, after having arranged to pick Tess up there the next day. She'd catch a ride in with Josie and then he could take her home after the appointment.

Crossing the street, he paused near the little red plywood shack that had somehow, magically, been transformed into Santa's house. Children were already lined up waiting to speak to Santa.

Nick studied them and their parents. No one seemed to find anything at all incongruous about a man in a red suit and the bright sunshine that poured down out of the clear blue sky. To them, this *was* Christmas weather.

Nick, too, had spent all his childhood Christmases in Southern California sunshine. He never thought twice about it—until, when he got older, his parents packed up the family and escaped to Tahoe for the holiday. Nick relished the snow and cold. Somehow, nothing was quite like twinkling snowflakes making lacy patterns on an icy window, or a cozy fire to warm you when you came inside. Even last year, when he got snowed in on a design job up in the Sierras, he loved it.

But there was no snow here. And hard as he tried, he could see no resemblance between the thin, balding man he'd met and the plump, white-haired figure who now sat in the big wooden chair, a little Oriental girl on his knee.

He leaned down, listening as she lispingly itemized her Christmas list, which seemed to include every toy advertised. Nick smiled at the innocent greed she displayed, remembering the days when he'd thought that life as he knew it couldn't possibly continue unless he had the latest battery-operated whizbang gadget he'd seen on television.

In a few years, he and Tess would be bringing their own son or daughter to talk to Santa, and no doubt he or she would have the same ridiculous urge to own everything. He hoped that it was something he and Tess would be doing together.

He was going to do his damnedest to see that it worked out that way. But it would only happen if it was what Tess wanted, too.

He laughed. Somehow, he never would've thought the first stop in rebuilding their relationship would be at an ob/gyn.

DR. KILDARE BORE no resemblance to Richard Chamberlain. She was a slender black woman in her forties, with a voice that seemed too deep for her build and eyes that inspired instant confidence.

Tess wasn't sure what she'd expected from Nick. A vague but uninformed interest at best. Boredom, at worst.

But he was showing no sign of boredom. Instead, he listened attentively as the doctor discussed the changes Tess could expect in the next month. At first Tess was acutely uncomfortable at finding herself in the midst of a very personal discussion of her body with Nick in the room. Not that he didn't know her body intimately, she reminded herself. But there was a difference.

This was a new level of intimacy. She'd never really thought about how closely entwined a man and woman became with the creation of a child. A part of Nick now dwelt inside her. It hadn't been quite real until the two of them sat down with the doctor and discussed the progress of that new life.

"Is everything going the way it's supposed to?" Nick asked.

"Tess and the baby are in good shape." Dr. Kildare's smile was understanding. She'd dealt with plenty of anxious fathers in her time. In fact, she preferred them to the ones who felt their duty ended at conception.

"There's nothing to be concerned about?" Nick probed, wanting to be sure. "Tess is awfully small, don't you think?"

Tess looked at him, startled by his obvious concern. She'd thought he'd be more concerned with the baby than with her, but that didn't seem to be the case.

"She's small but her pelvis is fairly wide. As the baby grows, we'll keep an eye on things. If there's any reason to be concerned, either for Tess's sake or for the baby's, we can always opt for a cesarean delivery. But I don't think it will be necessary."

Nick looked unconvinced but he didn't press the point. As they talked on, Tess hugged that concern close, feeling a warm glow in her chest.

And the concern didn't end when they left the doctor's office. Nick matter-of-factly told her she needed to get some solid food into her stomach and drove her over to dinner at Marie Callendar's. They got there early enough to beat the dinner crowd and were seated in a high-backed booth that provided an illusion of intimacy.

Their conversation ranged from disposable diapers—to which they both were opposed—to the possibility of world peace in their lifetimes—for which they both prayed.

Though Tess would never have believed it possible two days ago, when they left the restaurant she was pleasantly relaxed. She didn't even hesitate when Nick suggested taking the long way home so they could see the Christmas lights decorating people's homes.

"Want to check out the competition?" Tess teased him.

"I *have* no competition," Nick responded arrogantly.

Tess just rolled her eyes and laughed.

Days ago, she'd thought she might never see Nick again. Yet here she was, in the dark intimacy of his car, laughing with him.

But maybe she shouldn't be so surprised, she thought. The changes in her relationship with Nick had always come suddenly. From marriage to divorce to parenthood—none of it had been done at a reasonable pace. There had never been any time to stop and catch a breath.

They drove up and down the residential streets for almost an hour, admiring the decorations. It didn't matter whether it was just one long string of lights along the roofline or if the entire property was aglow from twinkling bulbs, they admired each and every one.

It was after nine when Nick pulled up to the curb in front of Tess's house. He walked her to the door, and went inside with her to flip on lights and make sure everything was all right. Tess was touched by his concern. Strangely, she'd missed that feeling of being protected.

"Would you like a cup of cocoa?" she asked, as she walked to the door with him. Since the question was followed by a yawn, it was hardly surprising that Nick shook his head.

"You need your sleep."

She wanted to argue but her body was telling her that he was right.

"I feel like Rip van Winkle," she grumbled, forcing back another yawn.

"You're much prettier than he was," Nick teased.

"Gee, thanks."

"Good night, Tess." His smile faded and he reached out almost compulsively, brushing his fingertips over the curve of her cheek. "Thanks for letting me go with you to the doctor's."

"You're welcome." Tess leaned her face into his hand, enjoying the faint roughness of his callused palm against her cheek. "I don't want to shut you out again. This is your baby, too."

"And a beautiful baby it's going to be." Nick's other hand settled on her stomach, his touch light through the fabric of her dress.

Tess felt his touch all the way to her core. It was always that way between the two of them. As if a fire lay waiting, ever ready to spring to crackling life.

"I want to kiss you, Tess." The words were not quite a question but Tess answered anyway.

"I want to kiss you, too." She leaned into his touch, her hands coming up to rest on his chest.

"Just a kiss. No more," Nick whispered, his mouth hovering over hers. "We're not going to rush into anything."

"No. We're not going to rush." Dimly she was aware of how foolish it was to say it when she could already feel the blood rushing through her veins, speeding her pulse.

Nick's hand slid from her face to cup the back of her neck as his mouth came down on hers. He might have intended the kiss to be only a warm good-night, a promise of what the future might hold for them. But the moment Tess responded, her slender body bending into his, her fingers sliding up his shoulders to tunnel into the thick blond hair at the back of his head, his intentions flew out the window.

His tongue swept the full line of her lower lip before dipping into her mouth, tasting the honeyed sweetness of her response. It was impossible to say that one was the match and the other tinder. The heat simply flowed between them, threatening to blaze out of control at any moment.

Nick's hand flattened over her spine, pressing her close to his hard frame as if he wanted to absorb her into himself. Tess could feel his arousal pressed against her stomach. The feel of it added to her own hunger.

She wasn't thinking about taking things slow. She wasn't thinking about anything but how right it felt to be in Nick's arms.

It was Nick who recognized the danger in what was happening. A dimly heard warning bell rang in his mind, far away but insistent. Wasn't this exactly what had caused them trouble in the past? It would be so easy to sweep Tess up in his arms, to carry her up the stairs and into the bedroom. She wouldn't offer a whisper of protest.

They both wanted it, he thought defiantly. They were consenting adults. Where was the harm?

The harm was in the inevitable regrets, afterward. It was in the feeling that they kept trying to build a relationship based on the undeniable sexual attraction between them. If he couldn't restrain himself even once, how could he expect Tess to believe him when he said that his feelings for her were more than physical?

But he wanted her and she wanted him.

His arms tightened around her but it wasn't enough to keep his thoughts at bay. Every instinct told him that to make love to Tess now would be a mistake—maybe the last one he'd get to make with her.

With a smothered groan, he dragged his mouth from hers. Setting his hands on her shoulders, he put her away from him, though he couldn't stop his fingers from caressing her arms.

Tess blinked up at him, her eyes all invitation. Nick ground his teeth together, feeling as if he were literally holding on to his willpower by the skin of his teeth.

"I don't want to screw things up this time, Tess," he said huskily.

Tess stared at him, her skin flushing as she realized how close she'd been to ending up in bed with Nick. Again. When she'd sworn not to. Again. And it hadn't been *her* common sense that had intervened.

She pressed her fingertips against her warm cheeks.

"Don't." Nick pulled her hands down, forcing her to meet his eyes. "Don't be embarrassed. I want you just as much as you want me. I can't hide how much I want you," he admitted ruefully.

Tess's eyes automatically dropped down his body, her cheeks flushing anew before she jerked her eyes away. But he'd succeeded in distracting her from her own feelings of embarrassment.

"There'll be other nights," he said, making the words a promise. "When we're sure."

He didn't wait for her response but drew her forward to press a quick, undemanding kiss on her mouth. Before Tess could respond, he was gone, the door closing quietly behind him.

Moving slowly, Tess twisted the dead bolt into place and then turned to lean against the heavy door. She stared into space.

She loved him.

The thought slipped in so quietly that she felt no real surprise when she realized it was there. Of course she loved him. She'd loved him from the moment they'd met. She'd never really stopped loving him, not even when she'd asked him for a divorce. It hadn't been Nick she'd doubted then. It had been herself.

Now, she'd proved she didn't need to doubt herself; she could survive on her own, succeed on her own. She didn't have to stand in anybody's shadow anymore. And now Nick had come back into her life.

She set one hand on her stomach, her fingers caressing the still-subtle bulge. Nick. A baby. A home for the three of them. Her business. Was it possible that she was going to be one of the lucky ones who had it all?

Of course, it was one thing for her to know she loved Nick. It was something else to know whether he loved her.

There could be no question he wanted her. But that wasn't love. There could be no question he wanted things to work out between them. But that was because of the baby.

No. Tess didn't want him to come to her because of the baby or because of an undeniable physical hunger. She wanted him to come to her because he loved her as much as she was finally willing to admit she loved him.

He'd loved her once. Was it possible he could love her again?

Chapter Eleven

"How do you feel about becoming an aunt?"

Hope Masters looked up from the salad she'd ordered, her startled green eyes meeting her brother's contained look.

"An aunt? What kind of aunt?"

"Are there different kinds?" Nick asked, amused.

Hope set her fork down and gave the question her full attention.

"Well, there's the adoptive sort of aunt—the ones who aren't related by blood. And there's the sort of ant that lives in holes in the ground and steals food at picnics. And then there's the sort of aunt that you become when your brother or sister has a child. I sincerely hope you're not talking about the last one."

"Sorry." Nick neither looked nor sounded apologetic. After last night, he wasn't sorry about anything. He was going to be a father and he and Tess were on the right track. This time, they were going to make it work. He could feel it in his bones. And he didn't think it would be very long before Tess knew it, too.

"Tess?"

"Who else?"

"She's pregnant?"

"That's what it usually takes for someone to become an aunt."

"Oh, Nick." Hope sat back against her seat, oblivious to the lunchtime crowd in the restaurant as she looked at her brother.

"You sound like I just told you that I have a fatal disease," Nick commented, not in the least disturbed by her reaction.

"Are you sure?"

"That I have a fatal disease?" he asked, raising his brows.

"That Tess is pregnant?" Hope brushed aside his attempt at humor.

"Absolutely. I'll be a father in May."

She started to speak, thought better of it and closed her mouth without saying a word. Nick sliced off a bite-size piece of chicken breast and put it in his mouth, giving his sister time to digest the news he'd just given her.

He'd finished that bite and was starting on another before Hope spoke again.

"Are you happy about this, Nicky?"

"Very. I didn't know I wanted to be a father until I found out I was about to become one. But now that I know, I couldn't be happier."

"Then I'm happy for you," she said, her tone more fitted to pronouncing death sentences.

"You certainly sound it," Nick commented dryly.

"I'm sorry." She picked up her fork and poked at her Chinese chicken salad without much interest. "I don't mean to sound gloomy. This has all been so sudden," she said fretfully. "I mean, one minute Tess has been out of your life for years. The next, you tell me you're seeing her again. And now she's expecting a baby."

"You sound just like Tess, complaining that things are going too fast."

"Well, much as I hate to agree with her, she's right."

"Sometimes things just happen that way," he said. "There's no rule about relationships having to take a certain amount of time to work."

"I didn't say there was, but I still think you're rushing things. I mean, a baby, Nick. You and Tess haven't even worked out the problems between you and you're going to have a baby. And after all the lectures you gave me about safe sex."

To his surprise, Nick felt his color mount. "I'm a little old for lectures, Hope."

"Apparently not. Really, Nick, how could you be so careless?"

"I don't have to justify my sex life to you," he snapped loudly. There was a momentary pause in the buzz of conversation near their table. Glancing around, Nick found himself the recipient of several discreet but interested looks. His flush deepened. He glared at Hope, laying the blame squarely at her feet.

She grinned heartlessly, amused to see her unflappable older brother blushing like a schoolboy caught in a misdemeanor.

"Before you were born, Bill MacDougal offered to trade me his brand-new bicycle for you, sight unseen. He thought having a baby sister would be fun. I should have traded you," he said regretfully.

"The bike would have worn out by now," Hope pointed out, unconcerned.

"Maybe. But it wouldn't have caused me near as much trouble before it did."

"It wouldn't have been half as much fun. And don't think that all this talk of Billy McNugget and bicycles is going to distract me from the subject."

"Billy MacDougal," he corrected. "And I know you well enough to know that nothing short of a nuclear blast could distract you once you sink your teeth into something."

"Thank you." Hope took this as a compliment, though his tone made it difficult to be sure he'd meant it as such. She bit into a snow pea and chewed thoughtfully.

"Are you and Tess going to get married again?"

"I don't know. I hope so but we haven't talked about it yet."

"Do you love her, Nick?"

She'd asked him that question once before and he'd told her that he didn't know the answer. Deep in his heart, he'd known he was lying even then. This time, he felt no such uncertainty.

"Yes. I do."

"Does she love you?"

Trust Hope to ask a difficult question, Nick thought ruefully. "I think she does. I'm not sure she knows it yet."

"Have you told her how you feel?"

"I don't think she's ready to hear it right now. I think she's as worried as you are about moving too quickly."

Hope pushed away her uneaten salad and fixed him with a worried look. "You know I want nothing more than to see you happy, Nicky. If Tess can make you happy, then I'll welcome her back with open arms. But if she makes you miserable again, I'm going to scratch her eyes out."

"Thanks. It's nice to know there's someone available to defend my honor."

"Anytime, Nick."

Nick glanced at the ticket the waiter had left and put enough bills on the tray to cover meal and tip. Hope slid out of the booth as he stood up. Slipping her arm through his, she pressed her head against his shoulder.

"Good luck, Nick. One way or another, you know Sara and Annie and I will make the best aunts any kid ever had."

NICK THOUGHT ABOUT her good-luck wishes a few hours later as he parked his car in the lot behind Tess's shop. Good luck. Did he need it? Was it gross overconfidence that made him think that Tess loved him as much as he loved her?

He'd seen her every day for the past week. They'd gone Christmas shopping together, wrapped gifts, picked out a small tree for Nick's condo. He knew it wasn't his imagination that they'd been some of the best times the two of them had ever had together. They'd talked and laughed and drawn closer together. Several times, he'd looked at Tess and seen love in her eyes.

Or had he only seen a reflection of his feelings for her?

Damn. Why did life have to be so complex?

Well, he certainly wasn't going to simplify it by sitting in his car, staring at her shop. He turned up his coat collar and stepped out into the drizzling rain—as close as L.A. ever got to a white Christmas.

Though it was after normal closing hours, the back door was unlocked. Tess had told him the shop would be open late and she'd explained why. But that hadn't been enough to prepare Nick for the shock of walking into Needles & Pins at nine-thirty in the evening and finding it full of customers. All male.

A men-only shopping night was an idea Tess had gotten from listening to her customers' complaints about the gifts their husbands picked out for them. It wasn't simply that men were inconsiderate louts who thought buying their wives a new food processor was the ultimate in thoughtful gift giving, though there were women who considered that a strong possibility. But part of the problem was that many of the things they really wanted were the sort of things that most men felt incapable of picking out.

So Tess had come up with the idea of a gift registry. It worked on the same principle as a bridal registry. Weeks before Christmas, women selected the items they wanted and wrote them on file cards. Tess kept the cards in the shop and the week before Christmas, Needles & Pins stayed open late one night—only to men.

Nick lingered in the back of the store, taking stock of the clientele. What had seemed at first to be a veritable horde reduced itself to fewer than a dozen men. But in the shop's narrow confines, that was enough of a crowd. It seemed to be a mixed bag. Wing tips mingled with construction boots. Brooks Brothers brushed shoulders with Levi's.

As Nick watched, Tess appeared from behind a rack of crewel kits. She was holding a white file card and talking to a burly construction worker who hung on her every word.

Nick shifted position slightly so he could keep an eye on things without drawing attention to himself. He enjoyed watching Tess work. He couldn't hear her but that didn't lessen the pleasure of watching her and knowing she was his. More or less his, anyway.

From the number of purchases Josie was ringing up, it was a safe bet that Tess's men-only night was a successful, and profitable, idea. It was also a tiring one, he thought, as he watched yet another customer approach Tess for help. Nick had been standing here for twenty minutes and she hadn't paused once.

"Do you know anything about needlework?" The question came from Nick's left, forcing him to drag his attention from Tess and turn it toward the man who'd spoken.

"Not much," Nick admitted.

"I don't know anything about it." He was about five foot eight and something less than twenty-five years old. From the way his shoulders filled his purple sweatshirt, it was a safe bet he was a weight lifter. In fact, he looked like nothing so much as a refrigerator with a head.

"Didn't your wife write down what she wanted?" Nick asked, glancing at the card the man was clutching.

"My mother," the younger man corrected gloomily. "She wrote down half a dozen things. How'm I supposed to know which one she wants?"

"Well, I'd guess if she wrote down more than one thing, any one of them would do."

But Refrigerator was already shaking his head. "Not my mother. I know her. There's five things here that she hates and only one she really wants. And if I don't pick the right one, then I don't love her."

A deep tuck appeared in Nick's cheek as he tried to suppress a smile he was sure would be unappreciated.

"What kind of needlework does she do?" Maybe they could narrow it down to the right technique and go from there.

"I don't know. She does stuff with yarn." He moved to a rack and stared gloomily at an array of counted cross-stitch charts. "She's always got something she's making. I don't know what she does with all of it. I mean, how many pillows can one house hold?"

Nick couldn't answer the plaintive question so he settled for nodding in a way that he hoped would look sympathetic.

"You have a mother?" Refrigerator asked, deep in gloom.

"Yes. But she plays golf and gardens."

"Lucky for you. What about your wife? She do this needle stuff?"

"My wife owns this shop," Nick said, his tone full of pride.

"Yeah?" For a moment, the cloud seemed to lift as he glanced around at the brightly lit shop. "That's impressive."

"She's an impressive woman."

The momentary distraction faded and Refrigerator turned back to the crumpled card. "At least you don't have to worry about buying her any of this stuff." With a sigh, he moved off to continue a quest he'd already deemed hopeless.

While they'd talked, they'd moved closer to the front of the store, and when Nick turned, he found himself face-to-face with Tess, who'd been standing right behind him. There was something in her eyes, a kind of surprised pleasure he didn't understand. He started to question it but Josie called her name. Tess gave him a quick smile and turned to answer and the moment was gone. But the look lingered in his mind.

IT WAS ALMOST eleven o'clock before Tess could close the shop. She hadn't had even one minute all night to talk to Nick.

The evening's drizzle had turned to a downpour and Tess didn't argue when Nick said he'd drive her home. The next day was Sunday and the shop was closed, so she wouldn't need her car first thing in the morning. Nick could bring her back to get it sometime during the day.

They didn't talk much on the drive home. Nick accepted her invitation to come in and share a cup of hot cocoa.

"Not the most exciting nightcap," Tess commented as she poured steaming milk over the mixture of cocoa and sugar she'd already measured into the cups.

"I've never had a better offer."

"I doubt that." The smile Tess threw him was tired but happy. "I've got marshmallows or whipped cream. Choose your poison."

"I think I'll have mine straight up."

"A purist. I guess I'll do the same."

She led the way into the living room and sank onto the sofa with a sigh. She took a sip from her cup. She'd always loved to drink cocoa around the holidays, regardless of the fact that the temperature rarely dipped below freezing. Tonight, though, it seemed the perfect drink to keep the chill and rain at bay.

Nick set his cup down on the coffee table and went to the Christmas tree. Reaching behind it, he plugged the lights in, bringing the tree to sparkling life.

"How about a fire?"

Tess hesitated only a moment, remembering what had happened the last time he'd built a fire. She nodded slowly. "That would be nice."

She watched as he crouched on the hearth and crumpled newspaper to use as a base for the kindling. He'd discarded his suit jacket and tie. His sleeves were rolled up to his elbows and his shirt was open at the throat. If she narrowed her eyes just a little, it wasn't hard to imagine that the cozy house was a log cabin they'd built themselves. The rain outside became a raging blizzard. They were snowbound till Christmas, isolated in the wilderness, with only themselves to depend on.

And she'd have felt every bit as safe and cared for under those circumstances as she did now, Tess thought. There was never a doubt about Nick's ability to cope under any and all conditions. He'd keep her dry and warm, and present her with a Christmas she'd never forget. Without being overbearing about it, Nick believed in protecting what was his. There was a part of her that was still uneasy in the face of his strength, but she was starting to believe that he could be strong without swallowing her up completely.

When the flames were licking up around the logs, Nick slid the screen into place and stood up, staring down into the fire for a moment before moving to join her on the sofa.

"Thanks for the help tonight," Tess said.

"Getting a box of bags out of the storeroom hardly constitutes a major contribution."

"Well, it was one thing Josie and I didn't have to do. Besides, I think just having you standing around looking calm helped some of the men. They tend to get nervous."

"It was easy for me to look calm. I didn't have to worry about choosing the right gift. You'd think with the choice narrowed down for them, it would make it simpler." Nick grinned at the memory of mangled cards and otherwise-competent men looking completely helpless.

"I think it's sweet that they care enough to worry," Tess said.

"If they worried less and trusted their instincts more, they'd have a lot less trouble making decisions."

Tess slanted him a sideways glance, acknowledging that it was probably difficult for him to understand that most people didn't trust their instincts the way he did. Nick believed in going with what his gut told him was right, whether it was buying a gift or marrying a woman he'd known for barely two months.

"That man you were talking to," she said slowly. "The one who was trying to find something for his mother."

"The one who looked like a refrigerator with a head?"

The description startled a smile out of Tess but it faded quickly.

"You told him that your wife owned the shop."

"Should I have said *ex*-wife?" he asked, turning to lay his arm along the back of the sofa, drawing his leg up on the cushion so that he faced her. "I didn't see any point in getting into semantics."

"It's not that." Tess waved one hand dismissively. "You said I'd done a good job with the shop."

"I said you were an impressive woman," Nick corrected her. Again, he saw that odd look of surprise come into her eyes.

"Do you really think that?" she asked tentatively. "You sounded almost... proud."

Nick's brows came together. "I *am* proud. You've done a hell of a job with that place. Most small businesses fail in the first year. You made it—and in spite of a soft economy. Of course I'm proud of you."

Tess looked down but not before he'd caught the sheen of tears in her eyes. He reached out and set his hand under her chin, tilting her face back up to his.

"Would you rather I wasn't proud of you?" he asked, bewildered by her reaction.

"No. Of course not." She sniffed back the tears. "I guess I never expected to do something that you'd be proud of."

"I was always proud of you," Nick said, his voice deepening.

"For what? Baking a good apple pie and needlepointing a pretty pillow?" Her tone scoffed at the possibility that she'd done anything to be proud of.

"Among other things." Nick had the feeling there was something important going on here, that he was on the verge of finding some of the answers he'd wanted five years ago. "You didn't have to do anything specific for me to be proud of you, Tess. You just had to be you. Sweet and giving and strong."

"But I never *did* anything," she said, seeming to think that explained everything.

"You didn't have to do anything. I loved you."

"But you were always doing things." She stood up, too agitated to remain seated. Nick rose more slowly, watching as she moved to stand next to the glittering tree. "Your whole family did things."

"Like what?" Nick couldn't remember anybody in the family doing anything extraordinary five years ago.

"You all had careers. You were going places and doing things."

"Mom's never worked in her life."

"But she's on every charitable committee in the state."

"If you wanted to do volunteer work, I'm sure she would have been happy to put you to work."

"You don't understand." She twisted her hands together, frustrated by her inability to make him see what she meant.

Nick caught her hands in his, stilled their restless movements. "Then make me understand, Tess."

She looked up at him looming over her and felt a totally illogical anger that he couldn't understand what was so obvious to her.

"You're so damned big," she burst out finally.

Nick's brows shot up. "I'm what?"

"You're big. You loom over me," she said crossly.

"Is that why you divorced me? Because I was too big?"

"Don't be stupid," she snapped. "Of course that wasn't why."

Completely bewildered, Nick stared at her, afraid to even guess at what she meant.

Tess sighed and tightened her fingers around his. "Look." Nick obediently lowered his gaze to their linked hands. "Look at the way your hand swallows mine."

"There's not a whole lot I can do about my size, Tess." But he was starting to get a glimmer of an idea as to what she was getting at.

"All my life, I watched my mother disappear in my father's shadow. Everything in her life revolved around him and his career. She was a pretty, intelligent woman, and when I was little she wrote poetry. Then my father told her that it was a waste of time and suggested that, if she wanted to write, she should try to do something for the base newspaper. Nothing controversial or too exciting. Officers' wives weren't supposed to be exciting. She threw her poems away, Nick."

Tess was unaware of the tears that had slipped from the corners of her eyes and were tracing silvery paths down her cheeks.

"She threw them in the trash and started writing a little column on household tips for the base newspaper. I was ten. When I asked her why she didn't write poems just for herself, she said that my father was right and that she'd been wasting her time.

"But he wasn't right," she said fiercely. "She had a right to have something for herself, to be something besides just his wife. I watched her let go of every one of her dreams for him. And he neither knew nor cared. He just accepted it as the way things should be."

"And you thought that you might do the same thing?" Nick questioned slowly. "That you might give up your dreams for me?"

"I swore I wouldn't be like my mother. I promised myself I'd never live in someone else's shadow."

"Who asked you to?"

The question startled her. Looking up at him, she was surprised to see genuine anger etching his features.

"I've got news for you, Tess," he continued without giving her a chance to answer him. "There isn't room for anyone in my shadow but me."

"You don't understand—" she began but Nick cut her off.

"I understand just fine. You're the one who's a little slow-witted about this." His fingers tightened over hers, refusing to let her withdraw. "Five years ago, you asked me for a divorce and I gave it to you because I knew you were unhappy. You didn't give me a decent explanation and I spent a lot of time wondering what I'd done. Now, I find out it had nothing to do with us at all. You were just trying to protect yourself from something that couldn't possibly happen."

"You don't know that," she protested.

"I've told you before, Tess, I'm not your father. And you're not your mother." He paused to let that idea sink in. "You took something that happened between two completely different people and applied it to us, twisting our relationship in your mind to make it fit your fears."

"It wasn't like that," she cried, reeling from the impact of his words.

"It was exactly like that," he said, his voice gentling at the shocked look in her eyes. "Tess, what happened between your parents had nothing to do with us. You didn't have to go off and make a success of your shop just to prove something to me. I already believed in you. What did you think I'd do if you told me you wanted to start your own business?"

"I...don't know." She was shocked to realize that she'd never really thought about it.

"So you just decided it would be safer to ask for a divorce?"

"I was scared," she admitted.

"So you ran. And we lost five years together." There was a wealth of sadness in his voice and Tess felt tears sting her eyes.

She stared at his shirtfront, trying to absorb the possibility that he was right, that her fears had cost them years of happiness and accomplished little else.

"I love you, Tess."

The quiet words brought her head up and her eyes met his in startled question. Nick released one of her hands, and his fingers brushed a soft tendril of dark hair back from her face.

"I loved you five years ago. I don't think I ever stopped loving you."

"Oh, Nick." The choked exclamation was all she could manage.

One small step brought her to him. His arms closed convulsively tight around her, drawing her closer still, holding her as if he'd never let her go.

"It's all right," he said. His lips brushed over her forehead. "We've got it straightened out now."

"Nick." Her hands clung to his shoulders as she tilted her head back. His mouth closed over hers, smothering anything else she might have said.

How was it possible that she'd lived so long without his touch? As his hand moved up and down the length of her spine, Tess thought vaguely that it was only in Nick's arms that she felt whole, only with his touch that she came alive.

Her mouth opened to him, her tongue coming up to twine with his. Her hands slid upward, her fingers delving into the thick gold hair at the back of his head as she rose on her toes, pressing herself to his broad frame.

She felt as if she needed to be so close that she was a part of him, so close that nothing and no one could ever pull them apart again. Tasting her hunger, Nick groaned low in his throat. One hand swept down her back, his fingers splaying over her firm derriere, crushing her to him.

Tess whimpered softly as she felt the hard ridge of him against her belly. Her head fell back, offering him free access to the slender length of her throat.

It was an invitation Nick didn't hesitate to take. His mouth slid downward, tracing the taut line of her throat with lips and tongue, sending shockwaves of pleasure throughout her body.

"Nick."

His name was a moan, a plea, an aching need.

He bent, one arm catching her behind the knees as he swept her off her feet and into his arms. Tess looped her arms around his neck, lowering her head to his shoulder as he carried her from the room.

He took the stairs as if her weight were nothing to him. Shouldering open the bedroom door, he carried her inside and stopped beside the bed before letting her slide slowly to her feet, the brush of her body on his a delicious torture.

Clothing whispered to the floor. Each touch, each caress was a promise for the future, a future they'd almost given up. Both felt conflicting urges—the need to rush to fulfillment contrasted with an equally strong need to savor every moment of this coming together.

Nick reached behind Tess and pulled down the covers before lifting her onto the bed. Light from the hallway splashed across the room, creating soft patterns of light and darkness.

Kneeling beside the bed, Nick set his hands on Tess's stomach, cradling the barely visible swell that marked where his child lay. His touch was tender, reverent, and Tess felt tears come to her eyes. How could she have thought to keep the knowledge of his child from him? How could she have failed to see how cruel it had been?

When he lifted his head to look at her, she raised her arms to him. He rose to lie beside her, keeping one hand on her stomach.

"God, Tess, I can't believe we're going to have a baby."

"I know. It seems like a miracle, doesn't it?"

"The miracle is having you back in my arms," he said, reaching up to brush her hair back from her forehead.

"It's being able to touch you like this again."

He bent to kiss her collarbone, stirring the fires to life.

"It's knowing you're mine."

Tess moaned as his palm closed over her breast.

"It's knowing you'll always be mine."

His mouth closed over hers, smothering anything she might have said. Tess's arms came up to circle his shoulders, her palms flattening on his back as he rose above her, his legs sliding between hers.

"I love you, Tess," Nick whispered against her throat. "I love you."

Tess caught her breath on a gasp of pleasure as he sank into her. She wanted to tell him she loved him, that she'd be his forever. But the words caught in her throat, drowned in a rising tide of pleasure.

But hadn't they always communicated best on this level? Maybe words weren't necessary, after all.

Chapter Twelve

"How about Ermingarde if it's a girl and Reginald if it's a boy?" Nick was leaning on the counter, watching Tess roll out pie crust for a mince pie.

"How about you don't try to publish a book of names for baby?"

"Okay, if you don't like Ermingarde and Reginald, what about Ophelia for a girl and Opie for a boy?"

"Opie? You want to name a child after Ron Howard?"

"No. I want to name a child Opie. I always liked that character. Little old ladies were always sneaking him ice-cream cones." Nick sounded wistful.

"Not Opie. And not Ophelia."

"Fine. Let's hear some of your brilliant ideas," he challenged.

Tess draped the crust over the rolling pin and carefully unrolled it over the filled pie pan. "How about Mickey for a boy and Minnie for a girl?"

"You laugh at my suggestions and then you want to name my son or daughter after a mouse?"

"Very successful mice." She slapped his hand as he tried to slip it under the crust to snatch some filling. "There's not going to be pie if you keep sneaking bites."

"But I love mince pie and nobody ever makes it except at Christmas. Besides," he said in a whiny tone, "I'm hungry."

Tess took one look at his fretful expression and burst out laughing. He looked so ridiculous wearing that petulant scowl.

"Laugh at me, will you?" Nick hooked his arm around her waist, swinging her off her feet and up against his chest. "You're a cruel, heartless wench."

"And you're too old to whine."

"Well, at least I don't have flour on my face."

"Where?" She wiped her hand over her face and saw Nick's eyes gleam with laughter as her flour-covered fingers spread a liberal dusting of white powder over her cheeks. Before he could duck, she wiped her hand over his chin, leaving a white trail.

"Brat."

"Fiend."

With each name they hurled at each other, they drew closer, until their mouths were only a breath apart. Once his lips touched hers, all game playing was abandoned. If Tess hadn't remembered the pie, Nick might have carried her upstairs immediately. He delayed only long enough for her to slide the pie into the oven.

The pie ended up with a charred crust. Nick could hardly complain since, as Tess pointed out primly, it was entirely his fault for distracting her.

"And," she said smugly, "you'll have to wait a whole year till next Christmas for me to make another one."

AFTER LUNCH THEY SLICED the pie and Nick consumed two large pieces, pronouncing it the best he'd ever eaten, char and all.

Outside, rain continued unabated. Inside, Nick had built a fire in the fireplace and they were settled in the living room with the glitter of the Christmas tree and the crackle of the fire holding the gloom at bay.

Nick was stretched out on the sofa, his head pillowed in Tess's lap. She stroked her fingers through his hair, watching the fire with dreamy eyes. It was hard to believe how everything had changed. Four months ago, she'd thought Nick was out of her life forever. Four months ago, the idea of having a baby had been a distant thing, postponed to the nebulous "someday."

"How did you feel when you found out you were pregnant?" Nick asked, seeming to read her mind.

"Happy. Scared. Confused."

"Happy?" He picked that emotion to question. "You were happy to be carrying my baby? Even then?"

"Yes."

The simple answer seemed enough to satisfy him. He turned his head so that his cheek rested against her stomach.

"Do you want a boy or a girl?"

"I don't care. As long as it's healthy."

"Me, too. Though I have to confess that a little girl who looked like her mother would be nice."

"No nicer than a little boy who looked like his father."

"Maybe we'll get one of each."

"Bite your tongue." She tugged a lock of golden hair. "One will do quite nicely, thank you."

Nick grinned but didn't bother to open his eyes.

Looking down at him, Tess was almost overwhelmed by a feeling of love. She couldn't imagine a more perfect moment than right now. Snuggled warmly in front of a fire with the man she loved next to her and his baby growing inside her. Tess knew nothing could ruin this moment.

"Mom's got a golfing buddy who's a justice of the peace," Nick said out of the blue. "I bet she could talk her into marrying us on Thursday."

Nothing could ruin this moment . . . except that.

Suddenly Tess felt her perfect moment shatter into a million pieces.

"What?" She struggled to keep her voice even.

"You know, she could pull a few strings for us by Thursday."

"Thursday?" The word stuck in her throat.

"Christmas Eve. Our old anniversary, remember?"

"I remember." She wasn't likely to forget her own wedding day. "Isn't that awfully soon?"

"It would be a rush," Nick said, mistaking her meaning. He opened his eyes and frowned up at the ceiling. "There wouldn't be time for anything fancy, but we'd be spending Christmas together as husband and wife."

Tess felt as if a hand had been clamped around her throat, threatening to cut off her air. This was Sunday and Nick was talking about getting married on Thursday. Four days. It was too soon. She hadn't had time to think, time to absorb all the changes.

She said nothing but Nick must have sensed something. He looked at her, his eyes searching. She didn't know what he read there but it was enough to cause his jaw to tighten. He sat up and swung around to face her.

"What's wrong?"

"It's awfully sudden, isn't it?"

"There doesn't seem much reason to wait, does there? I love you. You love me. At least, I assume you love me?" He made it a question and Tess suddenly realized that she hadn't said the words. Not last night and not this morning.

"Of course I love you, Nick." She reached out and he caught her hand in his. "With all my heart."

"Then why wait?" he asked. "I want to go into the new year with you as my wife, Tess. I want—I *need* to know that we're solidly together. I thought you'd want the same thing."

"It's not that. It's just…so sudden." She looked away. "Couldn't we wait?"

"How long?" His voice sounded restrained.

"I don't know. A few months, maybe?" She slid a quick look at him, reading his rejection even before he said anything.

"Tess, the baby will be born in a few months. Call me old-fashioned and hopelessly outdated but

I'd like to be married to my child's mother before he or she is born."

"A few weeks, then."

"Why wait?"

Why indeed? She stared at him, unable to come up with a single reason except the same old fears.

He must have read her answer in her eyes. His fingers tightened around hers for a moment and then released them.

"Please, Nick. Just give me a little more time."

"No." There was no give in him. "You either love me enough to trust me not to become like your father or you don't."

"I do love you!"

"But you don't trust me."

"It's not that."

"It's exactly that."

"I'm just not sure about getting married right away."

"When will you be sure?"

"I don't know," she cried, frustrated by her inability to explain the panic she felt.

Nick's jaw set to iron hardness. He stood up and peered down at her with eyes that were suddenly a bleak and wintry green.

"I'm not your father, Tess." Before she could utter the words on her tongue, he cut her off.

"Maybe you should consider that it takes two people to make a marriage, good or bad. Your mother made her choices, too. Just like you have to make yours." He turned toward the door.

Tess jumped up. "Where are you going?"

"I'm going home. I can't force you to trust me, Tess. If you decide you can, let me know and we'll go from there."

He walked out before she could frame a single sentence. Tess sank back down onto the sofa, staring at the door through which he'd disappeared.

"What happened?" she whispered aloud.

But the only reply was the crackle of the fire and the soft hiss of the falling rain.

TESS SAT THERE without moving, trying to absorb the rapid change in her life. It didn't seem possible that Nick had gone, that he'd walked out.

It had all been a misunderstanding. She'd only asked him for some more time. He couldn't have understood or he wouldn't have gotten so upset. It wasn't a matter of trust. It wasn't. She just needed a little time to adjust to the changes, time to be sure she was making the right choice.

The movement was so subtle at first that she almost didn't notice it, a tiny flutter, hardly stronger than the stroke of a butterfly's wing. It came again and she lifted her hand to her stomach, pressing her palm flat.

There it was again.

Her breath caught as she suddenly realized what was happening.

The baby was moving.

In the space of a breath, Tess's entire world shifted.

Her baby had just moved. The tiny life that was only just beginning to seem real had just made its presence known. There was a person inside her, a new life.

Tears burned her eyes but her mouth stretched in a foolish smile. She was having a baby. The statement was suddenly new and different. In a few months, there was going to be a new person in the world, someone completely different from either her or Nick.

Nick.

He should have been here. He should have been here to put his hand on her belly and feel this first tentative stirring.

The movement came again and Tess caught her breath on a half sob.

The realization struck her suddenly. What a fool she'd been. Nick had been right all along. It *had* been about trust, as much as it was about love.

She hadn't wanted to get married so soon because she hadn't really believed in him, hadn't really believed they could make it work. She had been trying to protect herself from being hurt by keeping a little distance between them.

She'd been looking to the past instead of to the future. But you couldn't feel the miracle of a new life stirring inside you without realizing that the future was all that really mattered.

And she'd just thrown it away.

SHE CALLED NICK'S apartment to tell him what a fool she'd been, but he didn't answer and she couldn't bring herself to leave a message on his answering machine. She kept calling until midnight but, if Nick was there, he wasn't picking up the phone.

By Monday morning, she'd convinced herself that he would never forgive her. He'd been hurt by her lack of trust and he'd never get past that. Oh, maybe he'd be civil enough. After all, there was still the baby to think about.

Unless he was so disgusted that he didn't want anything to do with her at all.

A healthy bout of tears accomplished nothing more than plugging up her nose and making her eyes water.

Reminding herself that she had a business to run, Tess mopped up the damage as best as she could and went in to open the shop, grateful that Josie wasn't coming in until after noon. By then, she'd have pulled herself together. She hoped.

It was just after eleven when the bell over the door rang, announcing the arrival of yet another customer. Tess looked up without much interest. The way she felt right now, she didn't particularly care whether she ever sold another skein of floss in her life. But she was interested in *this* customer.

Hope Masters.

Tess hadn't seen Nick's youngest sister in five years but there was no mistaking that tall, slim figure or that thick fall of pale gold hair.

"Hope. What a surprise." The banal greeting was all Tess could manage.

"You know, there was a time when I admired you, Tess," Hope began without preamble. "I thought Nick was lucky to have found you. And then you divorced him without a word of explanation to anybody and for a while, I actually hated you for hurting him."

She stopped and planted her hands, palms down, on the glass countertop. Everything about her stance was combative. Especially her eyes, dazzling with green fire.

"When Nicky told me he was seeing you again, I told him he was taking a big chance but I wished him luck. And when he told me about the baby and how he hoped to marry you again, I told him I'd welcome you back into the family, as long as you made him happy." Hope leaned over the counter, drawing her face just inches from Tess. "I also told him that, if you hurt him again, I would scratch your eyes out."

"Is that what you're planning on doing?" Tess asked, when Hope had to pause to draw breath. Tess held her ground, refusing to back away from the woman's hostile presence.

"I'd like to," Hope admitted bluntly. "But what I came here to do was to tell you that I think you're the blindest, stupidest woman on the face of the earth." She tapped a finger on the counter for emphasis. "Nick Masters is a terrific guy—and not just because he's my brother. Any woman can see what a great guy he is."

"I agree."

"Any woman would be lucky to have a man like Nick in love with her," Hope continued, oblivious of Tess's remark.

"I agree."

"Nick loves you and you used to love him."

"I still do."

"Nick—" Hope stopped mid-sentence and glared at her.

Tess's words had finally sunk in. Hope shook her head. "Then what the hell happened? How come Nick spent last night at my apartment, watching terrible old movies on cable and refusing to say anything except that I had a right to say that I'd told him so?"

"I'm the blindest, stupidest woman on earth," Tess said simply. "Just like you said."

Hope opened her mouth to argue, registered what Tess had said and closed it again. Her eyes reflected her confusion.

"You want to run that by me again?"

"I'm agreeing with you. I'm an idiot. Nick asked me to marry him again yesterday and I panicked for some stupid reason. He walked out before I realized how stupid I'd been. I called his apartment last night but I didn't get him. Now I know why."

"You admit you were wrong?" Hope asked, wanting everything clear.

"Absolutely. I love your brother more than anything on earth. I was going to go to his apartment tonight and see if he'd talk to me."

"You're too late," Hope said. "Nick left for San Francisco this morning to check on a project up there."

Tess felt tears sting her eyes. She'd been hoping—no, praying—that Nick could still pull those strings and arrange a Christmas Eve wedding.

"When will he be back?" she asked in a tiny voice.

"Christmas Eve."

Tess felt the words drive a knife through her heart. Christmas Eve—what would have been her second wedding day.

"I don't recall Nick mentioning anything about a San Francisco project." Tess was amazed she could even force words around the tightness that had formed in her throat.

Hope shook her head. "It's somebody else's design. Nick just wanted to get out. Said he needed a change of scenery."

Yes, Tess thought, *and I'm the scenery he wanted to change.*

"Look," Hope interrupted her thoughts. "You want to marry him, right?"

"More than anything." Tess forced a smile through the tears that now were spilling down her cheeks. "He wanted us to get married on Christmas Eve again. It seemed so quick." She shrugged. "Like I said, I panicked. I don't know if he'll be able to forgive me."

"Christmas Eve." Hope pinched her lower lip between thumb and forefinger, her eyes narrowed in thought. "It's just possible," she murmured.

"What is?"

"I've got to make some calls," Hope said abruptly, glancing at her watch. "Are you sure you love Nick?"

"Positive."

"And you'll do your best to make him happy?"

"Absolutely." Her sincerity must have been convincing because Hope suddenly smiled and it was like the sun breaking through storm clouds.

"Then I only have two things to say to you, Tess. One—you better dig out your wedding dress. And two—welcome back to the family."

And with that, Hope was gone in a swirl of poppy red slicker.

Tess had the feeling she'd been caught up in a tornado, spun around a few times and deposited in a foreign land.

She could only guess what Hope had in mind.

Whatever it was, she prayed it would be enough to convince Nick just how much she loved him.

NICK'S FLIGHT HAD BEEN delayed in San Francisco and he'd spent almost an hour sitting on the runway in an airplane packed full of people anxious to get home for the holiday. Ordinarily, he had as much Christmas spirit as the next man, but this year he could only wish the holidays over and done with. When some cheerful soul convinced the passengers that singing Christmas carols would help pass the time, Nick glowered out the window, feeling Scrooge-like and ill-tempered.

By the time his plane landed at LAX, he'd had all the good cheer and comradery he could stand. He wanted a stiff drink, a hot shower and a really terrifying horror novel, preferably one in which carolers were subjected to dreadful torments.

Hope had said she'd meet him and for once she was on time. Or maybe it was just that the flight had been late enough. Not even the sight of her smiling face did anything to lift his spirits.

"Merry Christmas Eve, Nicky." She threw her arms around him and gave him a hug. Nick returned the embrace but he couldn't manage much more than a grunt in response to the greeting.

"How was the trip?"

Discussion of the San Francisco job served to fill the time until they reached Hope's car. Nick was grateful for long-legged sisters who bought cars that didn't require a contortionist's skill to get into the seats. He slid onto the Cadillac's wide leather seat and dropped his head back with a sigh.

"Everyone's waiting for us," Hope said cheerfully.

Nick groaned. "Can't you just take me home and tell them my plane is missing somewhere over the Sierras?"

"Don't be a grouch, Nick. It's Christmas Eve."

As if he could forget, he thought, staring glumly out the window. He and Tess should have been getting married right about now.

"Thinking about Tess?" Hope asked, slanting him a sharp look.

"I shouldn't have rushed her," he said abruptly. "I should have given her the time she needed."

"Well, maybe you'll be able to straighten things out after the holidays," she said.

Nick threw her an annoyed look at her callous disregard for his feelings and then turned to look out the window. He subsided into brooding silence.

They didn't speak again until Hope pulled the car into the driveway of their parents' big home. Nick looked up at the sparkling Christmas lights and brightly lit windows and wondered how he could possibly get through the evening even pretending good cheer.

"Nick." Hope's tone was urgent and she caught his arm when he started to get out of the car. "You do love Tess, don't you?"

"For God's sake, Hope, leave it alone," he snapped.

"Do you love her?"

"Yes, dammit. Now I don't want to hear another word about her."

He stalked up to the front door, wondering what on earth was the matter with Hope. She wasn't usually so completely insensitive. When he pushed open the front door and stepped into the tiled entryway, the first thing that struck him was that the place was ablaze with lights. The second was that his entire family was gathered in the hallway, along with the minister from the church his parents attended and...Josie?

Nick felt his pulse start to beat a little faster. Behind him he heard Hope shut the door, then her soft murmur as she slipped past him to join the family. "Merry Christmas, Nicky."

He barely heard her. His eyes had been drawn upward. There was a woman descending the staircase. A woman wearing a tea-length ivory dress that he well remembered. She'd worn it seven years ago. He'd thought she looked like an angel then and the same thought occurred to him now.

"Tess."

As if walking in a dream, he moved toward her, meeting her at the foot of the stairs. She didn't descend the final step, so her eyes were level with his.

She swallowed, her eyes dark with uncertainty. "It's Christmas Eve."

"So it is."

"It's our anniversary."

"Yes."

She swallowed again. "I'm sorry for panicking."

"I'm sorry I was so pushy."

"Do you still want to marry me?"

"Only as much as I want to keep breathing."

He reached up, brushing his fingers through her hair, which she'd left down. "I love you, Tess."

"Oh, Nick. I love you, too. I felt the baby move and it made me realize what a fool I'd been."

"She moved?" His hand dropped to her stomach, pressing against the soft mound that held his child. In his eyes she could read his regret that he hadn't been there to share in the miracle. Tears stung her eyes and her smile shook around the edges.

"There'll be other times." She pressed her hand over his. "When I felt her move, it made me realize that I was looking only at the past when I should have been looking only at the future."

"Our future," he said.

"Our future. I trust you, Nick. I trust you with my heart. I trust you with our child. I trust you with my future."

"Without you, there is no future." He smiled slowly into her eyes and leaned forward, sealing their words with a kiss.

In a moment they'd exchange their vows and seal those with another kiss. But these were the first and most important promises they'd exchanged this night.

Tess put her arms around his neck, knowing she'd come home at last.